"It…unfastens…in the…front."

Within seconds Chance had unclasped her bra, and began stroking Tiffany's breast.

A streak of sunlight fell on his face, lighting up a killer smile that branded him ready for anything.

As any good-time guy should be.

"You're so…beautiful," he rasped against her mouth before lowering his to one bare breast, then to the other.

She closed her eyes, savoring the feel of him. Wanting more. Wanting him.

"I think…" she began just as he nipped gently. She almost screamed in pleasure.

"What do you think?" he asked.

"I think," she began again, knowing she'd had a point but couldn't recall it. He moved restlessly against her and she quickly remembered. "That we should get naked."

"Excellent suggestion," he said, lifting his hips and shucking his pants and underwear so swiftly that she had to laugh.

Dear Reader,

I've always wanted to be the kind of person who takes chances. Wild, daring chances like leaping out of airplanes, scaling majestic mountains and acting on my impulses. Unfortunately, I'm a conventional girl.

So is Tiffany Albright, the heroine of *One Hot Chance*. But Tiffany is fed up with not only the staid life but also the parade of boring men she meets as a Washington, D.C., lobbyist.

I thought it would be fun to explore what happens when Ms. Conservative gathers her courage and takes a chance on a stranger she thinks can show her a good time.... Except Chance McMann is not what he seems.

One Hot Chance is my first book for Harlequin Temptation after six stories with Harlequin Duets. Hey, maybe I am unconventional after all!

Enjoy!

Darlene Gardner

P.S. Online readers can visit me at www.darlenegardner.com.

Books by Darlene Gardner

HARLEQUIN DUETS
39—FORGET ME? *NOT*
51—THE CUPID CAPER
68—THE HUSBAND HOTEL
77—ANYTHING *YOU* CAN DO...!
101—ONCE SMITTEN
     TWICE SHY

Don't miss any of our special offers. Write to us at the following address for information on our newest releases.

Harlequin Reader Service
U.S.: 3010 Walden Ave., P.O. Box 1325, Buffalo, NY 14269
Canadian: P.O. Box 609, Fort Erie, Ont. L2A 5X3

One Hot Chance
Darlene Gardner

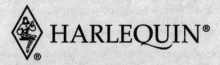

HARLEQUIN®

TORONTO • NEW YORK • LONDON
AMSTERDAM • PARIS • SYDNEY • HAMBURG
STOCKHOLM • ATHENS • TOKYO • MILAN • MADRID
PRAGUE • WARSAW • BUDAPEST • AUCKLAND

To my husband, Kurt,
for those sultry Savannah nights of our past.

ISBN 0-373-69126-2

ONE HOT CHANCE

Copyright © 2003 by Darlene Hrobak Gardner.

This edition published by arrangement with Harlequin Books S.A.

® and TM are trademarks of the publisher. Trademarks indicated with ® are registered in the United States Patent and Trademark Office, the Canadian Trade Marks Office and in other countries.

Visit us at www.eHarlequin.com

Printed in U.S.A.

1

THE NIGHT WAS MOON-BRIGHT, pulsing with life from the crowd packing the cobblestone street and teeming with possibility.

Tiffany Albright watched a young man throw back his head and howl at the moon before he joined a triumvirate of fraternity boys, proudly brandishing their Greek letters and plastic cups of green beer.

She hooked her right arm through Susie Dolinger's left and sighed with pure delight.

"Visiting you the week of the St. Patrick's Day festival is the best thing I've done in a long time," Tiffany said.

Susie dodged a couple who'd stopped ahead of them to share a passionate kiss and frowned, which wasn't one of her typical expressions. With her blond curls, dimples and sunny disposition, she usually reminded Tiffany of a grown-up Shirley Temple.

"I don't know about that, Tiffany, honey. When I said you should come to Savannah, I surely didn't mean now. I'll be too busy this weekend to spend much time with you and besides..."

Her voice trailed off and Tiffany shot her a curious glance. Susie, who'd been her best friend in high school until the State Department had moved her father and the rest of the family to Australia, had returned to her native Savannah three years ago. In that time, she'd invited Tiffany to visit no less than a dozen times.

"Besides what?" Tiffany asked.

Susie sighed. "I thought you'd like the sleepy Savannah." She gestured at the crowd around them with a sweeping hand. "Not this one."

Made up of the cobblestones that were once the ballast stones in sailing ships, historic River Street boasted restaurants, pubs, hotels and tourist shops housed in the cotton warehouses and offices of the 1800s. A collection of small parks and sitting areas across the street provided up-close views of the Savannah River and the huge ships that continually went to and from the port.

Susie said the street was never quiet. It was Thursday night, a full twenty-four hours before the festival weekend would really get rolling, but the crowd was already nearly large enough to rival the one at Times Square before the ball dropped.

"What's wrong with this Savannah?" Tiffany asked as two men in their twenties with their arms flung around each other's necks walked by singing a rousing rendition of "When Irish Eyes are Smiling."

"Not a darn thing. I work for the Bureau of Tourism, remember? But I can't help thinking you'd prefer the other Savannah."

The sleepy, Southern, boring one.

"And why's that?" Tiffany tried to keep her voice light. She really did.

Susie squeezed her arm. "Don't go getting offended on me. It was a compliment. I only meant the city goes wild this weekend and you're so...conservative."

"I am not!"

"You're the daughter of an old-fashioned Iowa politician who's been in Congress for more than twenty years."

"That only proves my father is conservative, not that I am."

"You live in Washington, D.C., work on the Hill as a lobbyist and go to $1,000-a-plate dinners. If you're not conservative, then I don't know an azalea from a magnolia."

Tiffany unhooked her elbow from Susie's and folded her arms across her chest as she walked. It hurt that Susie, of all people, saw her that way. Hadn't Susie realized while they were attending the exclusive D.C. private school together that Tiffany had gravitated toward her precisely because she livened up the atmosphere?

"Did it ever occur to you that I might be tired of that kind of life?" Tiffany asked. "That I might be ready to let loose and go wild?"

A preteen whose parents were nowhere in sight blew into a plastic horn as he passed them. Tiffany jumped at the noise, barely refraining from squealing.

Susie laughed. "No."

"Just because I react normally to sudden sounds—"

"It's not that. It's everything else," Susie interrupted. "Why, it's even the way you're dressed."

"I'm dressed in green!"

"Do you really think a wild woman dresses in an emerald-green designer pantsuit tailored expressly for her?"

"I have problems getting clothes off the rack that fit," Tiffany said defensively. "I happen to be five foot ten."

"Is that a conservative estimate or your true height?" Susie asked.

Tiffany started to take affront but then her friend laughed and the outrage drained out of her. She laughed too and hooked her arm once again through Susie's.

"Okay, okay. I may not be Ms. Nonconformity but I was going to do something drastic if I didn't get out of D.C."

"Like what? Tell somebody you didn't like his tie?"

"I was thinking more along the lines of squeezing really hard the next time a politician shook my hand and gave me an empty smile. Or dumping my drink on any attorney who made a self-serving comment. But then my hand would be sore from all the squeezing and I'd be exhausted from going to the bar to get my drink refilled."

"It can't be that bad."

Tiffany lifted her face to the soft breeze, which felt wonderful after the day's heat even if it did carry the faint scent of beer. Although only March, the temperature had reached eighty-five earlier that day and had yet to dip below seventy.

"Lately, it has been that bad. I feel so...trapped. My

mother's taken to trying to match me up with every Starched Suit in town."

Susie scrunched up her small, pert nose. "Isn't the usual expression Stuffed Shirt?"

"Starched Suit fits these guys better. Most of them wouldn't take off their jackets during a heat wave in hell. Talk about boring, they could put a humming-bird on caffeine to sleep."

Susie giggled.

"What I need is somebody like your Kyle," Tiffany said. "Somebody who doesn't fit the suit-and-tie mold. I mean, Kyle's a freelance photographer. How cool is that?"

"Very cool," Susie said.

"I wouldn't need him for long," Tiffany said consi-deringly, letting her fantasy take hold. "Just for the weekend."

"Sorry to break this to you, honey." Susie's voice was mild but her eyes had grown wide and horrified. "But Kyle's taken."

"I wasn't talking about Kyle specifically, silly," Tif-fany said, batting lightly at her arm and laughing. "He's completely taken with you, as well he should be. I was talking about some anonymous good-time guy I could spend the weekend with."

"Please tell me you don't mean sexually," Susie said, still wearing that look of dismay.

Tiffany thought about that for a moment. For all of her twenty-seven years, she'd acted the part of the good girl: doing well in school and career; fulfilling the endless social obligations required of a congressman's daughter and then a lobbyist; acting as though her insular little world was all she needed.

She'd begun to despair she'd spend her entire life in business clothes and panty hose, smiling at dull men until her face hurt.

"Sure," Tiffany said slowly. "Why not sexually?"

"Because..." For a moment, Susie was uncharacteristically speechless. "Because you're not that kind of girl."

"Maybe I am that kind of a girl," Tiffany said, tossing her long, dark hair defiantly. She suddenly had the strange feeling that she didn't know where she fit into the world. "How can I know what I like if I don't experience it?"

"But...but..." Susie sputtered. "You don't have to experience something to know it's not for you. Like...skydiving. Can't you look up at a plane and tell you don't want to jump out of it?"

"Maybe I would like to take the leap," Tiffany said.

"No, you wouldn't," Susie countered.

"Maybe I was talking about leaping into bed with someone instead of leaping out of a plane."

Susie shook her blond head. "You don't mean that. I know you. You're not the type to have an affair."

"I don't want to have an affair," Tiffany said decisively. "I want to have a fling."

Somewhere someone in the crowd whooped, a long, gleeful note that pierced the night air. Tiffany threw back her head as she'd seen the young man do not long before but couldn't bring herself to howl at the moon. She did, however, manage to giggle.

"You've gone crazy," Susie said.

"And it's about time I did." Tiffany felt a surge of adrenaline shoot through her veins. Yes, she'd have a fling. It was a wonderful idea.

"It's a terrible idea," Susie said. "You can't pluck some man off the street and have a fling with him."

"Isn't that what you did with Kyle?" Tiffany asked.

Susie's fair complexion suffused with color. "I never should have told you that story. And we didn't meet on the street. We met in a bar."

"Maybe that's where I'll meet my fling guy," Tiffany said happily. "Savannah has lots of bars, doesn't it?"

"Don't you go forgetting it also has its fair share of drunks, especially at festival time."

"I'm not going to pick up a drunk," she said. "I'm going to choose somebody wonderful. I have excellent instincts about people."

Susie checked her watch, then cast a worried glance at Tiffany. She breathed out a heavy sigh. "My timing's rotten as usual. I'm due at the main stage to make sure the next act runs smoothly."

"Then go."

"I'm not sure I should leave you alone." Susie's fair eyebrows drew so close together they nearly tangled. "You don't seem to be in your right mind."

"Don't worry about me." Tiffany gave her friend's arm a pat. "I promise not to do anything that doesn't feel right."

Susie's frown deepened when Tiffany let out another giggle. "That's exactly what I'm worried about," Susie murmured.

2

CHAUNCY "CHANCE" McMANN slipped his right hand into the pocket of his expertly tailored navy-blue suit so he wouldn't thump the polished wood of the hotel registration desk with it.

He'd long ago decided to let intellect rather than emotion rule his actions.

"There must be some mistake," he said, using the tried-and-true eye contact that had made him a successful corporate litigation attorney. "My travel agent reserved a room for today and Friday. If you check your computer again, I'm sure you'll find the reservation."

The female clerk had dark, expressive eyes. Chance couldn't have said whether she was pretty because she'd been mysteriously holding her left hand in front of her face since he'd approached the front desk.

"I'll be happy to check that for you again, sir." She used the fingers of one hand to tap at the keyboard of the computer in front of her. The machine looked out of place in the old-world elegance of the lobby, which was richly decorated with wood-paneled walls and emerald brocade furniture. "I'm sorry, but I still don't have a record of the reservation. And unfortunately, we're fully booked."

Chance barely stopped himself from groaning aloud at this latest piece of bad luck. Since he'd left Washington, D.C., earlier that afternoon, the airline had lost his luggage, all the rental agencies were out of cars and his clothes...well, he didn't even want to think about his clothes.

"I know this is asking a lot," Chance said, using his most persuasive smile, "but could you possibly call some other hotels to see if they have a room."

The clerk, her left hand still shielding her face, seemed to lean away from him.

"I'm afraid that won't do any good. I called round a little while ago for another gentleman and there's not a vacancy in the city." Her dark eyes appeared genuinely regretful as she lifted her slim shoulders in a shrug. "It's always like this at festival time."

"So I gathered," Chance muttered. "Could I ask one more favor? Could you call the airport to see if I can get a flight back to Washington, D.C., later tonight?"

While the young woman made the call, curiously keeping her back to him, Chance tamped down his irritation.

As a lawyer who packed his weeks with work, he didn't have time for this. He'd come to Savannah as a favor to Georgia congressman Jake Greeley, a friend not only of his father's but also of a senior partner in his new law firm.

Chance had left Atlanta a month ago for D.C. and the prestigious new firm, but he still had a license to practice law in Georgia. That made him the logical choice to discreetly handle a legal matter that had arisen from a traffic dispute involving Greeley's daughter.

It should have been simple enough. But now it seemed Chance would have to return to D.C., postpone the meetings he had scheduled for tomorrow and fly back to Savannah next week.

"There's a flight that leaves at ten o'clock, which is about three hours from now," the clerk said after she hung up the phone. "There are plenty of available seats so you should have no problem booking it when you get to the airport."

"Thank you," he said, but the clerk's hesitant throat clearing stopped him before he could turn to go. He regarded her questioningly.

"I don't mean to be rude," the clerk said. Behind her hand, he could tell that her nose was wrinkled. "But, well, did you know there's something splattered on your suit? At first I could have sworn it was mud, but it sure smells like—"

"It *is* mud," Chance said, which is what he'd been telling himself since he'd gotten out of a taxi and a shuttle bus had splashed him with the contents of a gutter.

Even though horses pulled carriages full of tourists through the Savannah streets, his mind refused to consider the other possibilities.

After all, a city ordinance did require the horses to wear diapers.

"Thanks again for your help," he said and hurried out of the stately inn in search of new clothes.

Ten minutes later, after rummaging through the

pile of kelly-green T-shirts on a table in a cramped novelty store, he picked up one and headed for the cashier's counter.

He waited patiently through purchases of a green fright wig by a middle-aged woman and a green beret by an elderly man before he reached the front of the line.

"Do you have any more of these?" He gestured to the T-shirt he held. "This was the only large on the table."

"You sure are lucky you found a large then." The clerk rested her plump hands on the counter. She was a round-faced, slow-talking woman with beauty-shop perfect gray hair. "Those shirts have been selling like water bottles in hell."

"Are you *sure* you don't have any more?" Chance wouldn't have persisted if he hadn't been desperate, but Savannah Smiles was the only store he'd found that sold clothing of any kind. The shops of River Street, however, *were* a fine place to find hand-crafted jewelry, regional artwork and Civil War memorabilia.

"Wouldn't have said so if I wasn't sure." The clerk rubbed her short, turned-up nose. "Honey, what is that all over your nice suit?"

"Mud," Chance answered quickly.

"You sure? Because it sure st—"

"Look, I'm in a bind here," he interrupted. "I really need to buy a shirt."

"That one will cost you twenty dollars, on account of it being festival time," the cashier said, getting ready to ring up the sale.

"But not this shirt," Chance said.

"Hey, mister, would you make up your mind already," came a voice from the back of a line that was now three people deep. "I got some serious drinking to do."

"I don't understand why you don't like that shirt you got there," the clerk said.

Chance held it up, displaying the saying stenciled across it in bold black letters: Irish You Would Kiss Me.

"Do you understand now?" he asked.

The clerk had the audacity to laugh. "That's about the most clever thing I ever did see," she said. "Why don't you let me ring it up for you so these good people behind you can be on their way?"

After giving into inevitability, Chance used the closet-size store bathroom to change out of his ruined clothes and emerged once again onto River Street. In addition to the tacky shirt, he wore the lightweight sweatpants and running shoes he'd tossed into his carry-on bag at the last moment.

Figuring there was never a bad time to conduct business, he found an empty bench and pulled out his cell phone. Congressman Greeley wouldn't be happy about the delay, but neither was Chance. He'd cleared his calendar through Monday, which hadn't been an easy feat, and it was all for naught.

Ignoring the distractions around him, he left word on three separate answering machines that he couldn't make tomorrow's meetings and would be in touch soon to reschedule. Then he dropped the phone back in his bag and joined the flow of tourists on the street.

It didn't take long for someone to remind him of what was stamped across his T-shirt.

"Smooch, smooch," a scantily dressed teenage girl called to him. She pursed her lips, then buried her laughing face in the shoulder of a friend.

"Come over here and I'll plant one on ya," the friend added and the two girls erupted into giggles.

Chance rolled his eyes and checked his expensive gold watch. He had at least an hour before he needed to head for the airport, but no way was he spending it on River Street.

He was about to flag down a taxi when he remembered the intriguing glimpses he'd gotten of the city's residential section on the drive from the airport.

Making a snap decision, he walked away from the waterfront and dodged traffic as he jaywalked across Bay Street toward the heart of the city. The waste of time nagged at him but not for long. By the time he reached the second of the city's series of squares, he was charmed.

They consisted of miniature parks surrounded by houses, churches and businesses. Cypress and elm trees swept above the sidewalks, lending an elegant shading to a night scented with jasmine from the fragrant blooms decorating the landscape.

It was less crowded here, but people still walked about as though it were broad daylight. Lights blazed from magnificent homes with architecture distinguished by wrought-iron balconies, fences and fancy ornamental work. Many of them housed parties with laughter and music spilling onto the street.

"Irish you would kiss me, too," said a tall man in a wig and a tight dress, blowing him one from ruby-red lips. "You are simply divine."

"Thank you," Chance said, oddly flattered. Chuckling to himself, he walked on until he heard a saxophone treating the night with a familiar, jazzy tune.

He smiled as memories washed over him. He'd practiced that same song over and over again when he was sixteen, initially to impress Lyndsey Ellicot, the prettiest girl in tenth grade.

It turned out Lyndsey didn't like jazz, but Chance was hooked. At least until school and work and life took over, and he realized his father was right. He didn't have the time to indulge himself with the sax. Or Lyndsey, not that it had mattered by then.

He let the bluesy notes drift over and through him as he gravitated toward the musician, who looked like he should be playing football instead of jazz. When the song ended, he showed his appreciation with three loud hand claps.

"You do John Coltrane proud," Chance told him. "If I'd closed my eyes, I'd have sworn I was listening to him."

The other man gave him a smile as wide as the Savannah River, revealing two gold-capped front teeth. "Most folks woulda guessed that was Charlie Parker."

"Nope. That's Coltrane. Used to play those numbers myself," Chance said, the nostalgia making his voice wistful.

"Hot damn." The man held the instrument out to him. "Then you got to play something, too."

"Oh, no," Chance said, shaking his head.

"You afraid of germs?" The man lifted the end of his gray T-shirt and gave the mouthpiece a swipe before Chance could answer. "There. No more germs."

Chance laughed. "I'm not afraid of germs."

"Then what?"

He started to explain that he wasn't the kind of man who played the sax on a balmy Savannah night where anybody walking by could hear.

Hell, he didn't play at all anymore. He litigated cases.

"Well," the musician asked, the instrument still outstretched. "You gonna play or aren't you?"

The streetlight caught the brass of the instrument, making it shine like one of those lucky pennies he never had time to pick up. What the hell, Chance thought. Nobody would ever know.

"You're on," he said.

AN HOUR AFTER TELLING HER friend she was in the market for a fling, Tiffany walked alone through the residential streets of historic Savannah in the direction of Susie's place.

She hadn't said a word to anyone except a swaggering blonde in his mid-twenties, handsome except for the leer on his face, who'd asked, "Hey, babe, wanna get lucky?"

"No, thank you," she'd answered primly without breaking stride.

The men strolling River Street who weren't part of a couple, and some of those who were, seemed to consider getting sloshed the equivalent to having a good time.

She checked the face of her slim, gold watch, which showed it wasn't yet eight o'clock. She puffed up her cheeks and blew out a breath.

Susie didn't know how right she was.

Not only wasn't Tiffany the kind of girl who had affairs, but she was also the kind of girl who went home early to go to bed with a good book.

The wail of a saxophone drifted through the square, its melancholy tune mirroring her mood. She walked in the direction of the sound and joined the small crowd that had gathered around the dark-haired, lean-hipped street musician playing the instrument.

Her mouth went dry at her first good look at him, and she had a crazy, fervent hope that she was the kind of girl who picked up men after all.

His eyes were shut as he blew out the notes and moved with the music as though it lived inside him. He couldn't have been more than an inch or two taller than she was, but the combination of moonlight and streetlight made him appear magnified.

His hair was probably brown but it appeared golden in the glow of the moon, as did his eyelashes, which were thick against his tawny skin. What she could see of his face made her think of sin and delight.

And his body...oh, his body was a thing of beauty.

It wasn't so much the shape of it, although there was nothing wrong and quite a lot right with lean and muscular. It was the way he moved.

She could imagine that body poised above hers, moving inside her.

He shifted, the motion stretching the fabric of his green T-shirt over his broad shoulders. Her eyes dipped and she read the caption on his shirt: Irish You Would Kiss Me.

A shiver passed through her.

The last jazzy notes of the song faded into the night, and the street musician seemed to emerge from his trance as he pulled the instrument from his mouth. Then he smiled.

The smile was electrifying, an unrestrained grin that hinted at the heart of a rebel. It lit up his face, highlighting features that otherwise might have seemed ordinary.

But there was nothing ordinary about the way her pulse rate kicked up when he lifted his eyes and met her gaze. Dimly she was aware of another man taking the saxophone from him, freeing his hands. For her?

Don't be a coward, she told herself. *He's exactly what you've been searching for.*

She took a step—and noticed that his hair wasn't golden but dark brown, his eyes an intriguing shade somewhere between green and blue. The eyes of a sorcerer, she thought. One who'd already begun weaving a spell. Excitement coursed through her veins along with her blood, and she took another step. Another. And yet another.

All the while, her eyes were locked on his. She wondered what would happen when she got close enough to touch him, if he would put into words what was happening between them.

Let loose. Go wild.

That's what she'd meant to do before her feet had gotten so cold they were in danger of frostbite. That's what she'd be doing if she kissed this sexy stranger.

It's only one kiss, she told herself.

One kiss. The words pulsed inside her brain along with three others: *Go for it.*

His dark-brown head tilted inquisitively at her approach and she noticed that his mouth was still red and moist from playing the sax. Oh, Lordy.

She wasn't sure whether it was nerves or excitement that caused her pulse rate to spike as she leaned toward him. The clean, intoxicating scent of his skin seemed to urge her closer. Surprise flashed on his face but he didn't budge, making it easy for her to touch her mouth to his.

She intended to draw back after the briefest contact, but she felt the heat she'd seen in his eyes searing through her like a flash fire. Felt it and tasted it against her lips, which were suddenly clinging to his as though indulging a craving.

She felt dizzy with the pleasure of it, and the hands she'd intended to place on his chest to hold him at bay snaked up and around his broad shoulders and hooked around his neck. Her fingers settled in his hair, which felt like heated silk.

And then he was returning the kiss, slanting his

mouth over hers, linking his hands at her waist to pull her close. His body was hard, but she was going soft and pliant as a honeyed heat settled low in her stomach and spread out like a fan.

Her tongue flickered out, touched his and elicited pleasure so intense she nearly moaned with it. She could have gone on kissing him forever, might have if he hadn't winced. Confused, she pulled her mouth from his.

"Ow," he said.

It took her a moment to realize she had stepped on something and that the full weight of her body was bearing down on it. She looked down to see what it was.

It was his toe.

She sprang back from him, feeling a flush creep up her neck. Some temptress she was. It'd be a wonder if he wasn't tempted to tell her to go away.

"I'm sorry," she said in a breathy voice she barely recognized.

"That's okay." A slow smile arched the lips that had curved lovingly around the sax. Like her, he seemed short of breath. "You can step on my toe anytime you like."

His voice was deep and seemed to cascade over her skin, like flowing honey. Somehow, it renewed her courage.

"Actually, I didn't come over here to step on your toe," she said softly, her eyes once again locked on the sorcerer's blue-green of his.

"I figured that," he said, one corner of his sexy mouth kicking up.

She felt her flush deepen and had the overwhelming sensation that she should explain herself. Her eyes flicked to the saying on his shirt.

"It's your own fault," she said. "Wearing a shirt like that. Why, anybody could walk up to you and try to kiss you."

Great, she thought in disgust. She'd gone from a femme fatale who crushed toes instead of hearts to a member of the decency police warning him that a lecherous public was on the prowl.

"You mean," he asked, his eyes focusing on her lips, "like you did?"

"Exactly." She gulped. He didn't seem turned off by either the scolding or the toe crushing. "I took you at face value. I didn't even ask how you felt about strange women kissing you."

That beautiful mouth parted—in amusement?

"I'm in favor of strange women kissing me," he said, his eyes still locked on hers. "The question is how you feel about strange men kissing you?"

She tapped a finger against her lower lip, partly to fool him into thinking her calm and collected but mostly to get it to stop trembling.

"I hadn't thought about it much," she lied. "But I suppose it would depend on the strange man."

In the course of their conversation, neither one of them had moved away. The difference in their heights was so slight their eyes were nearly level.

His were hot. So very hot. Like licks of flame.

"I know where you can get a shirt like this," he whispered and she felt his breath against her lips. "Then you can conduct your own experiment."

She moistened lips that had suddenly gone dry. "Or you can pretend I'm already wearing one," she whispered back.

Amusement danced in those hypnotic eyes as the air seemed to crackle around them.

"Works for me," he said before he cupped the back of her head and captured her mouth with his.

Because she'd tasted him once, she didn't hesitate in opening her mouth, inviting him to plunder instead of tease. He immediately obliged, erotically tangling his tongue with hers.

She might have suspected the sensations that swamped her the first time they kissed had been a fluke if they hadn't consumed her again. Liquid heat poured through her, making her knees feel so rubbery she had to grip his shoulders and hold on.

No man had ever made her feel this way with a mere kiss, she thought dimly as she angled her head in a desperate attempt to get even closer to him.

No man had ever made her feel this way at all.

He made her blood hum, her ears fill with music. Except that couldn't be right, especially because the music not only had a recognizable melody but sounded suspiciously like it was coming from a saxophone.

With a supreme effort, she broke off the kiss and drew back in his arms. She was so breathless she could barely speak. "Please tell me that's not 'Hold Me, Thrill Me, Kiss Me.'"

"Okay." His eyes were half-lidded, his skin slightly flushed, revealing he'd been as affected by the kiss as she was. "But it is."

When she'd stumbled across him playing the sax, no more than a half-dozen people had been gathered around him. She took a peek and saw there were now easily twice that many. At least half of them were clapping.

She buried her face against his shoulder, which felt strong and solid against her heated cheek. "That applause is for us, isn't it?" she whispered against the green fabric of his T-shirt.

"They probably think we're street performers," he said into her ear, eliciting another shiver. "Acting out the lyrics to that song."

"Can't you get your sax back and make him stop?"

"I could if it were my sax."

The instrument wasn't his? Tiffany would think about that later, but now she had a more pressing problem. "What should we do?"

She felt his chest rumble with low laughter. "Can you do a backbend?"

She raised her baffled eyes to his dancing ones. "Sure, I guess."

Almost before she'd finished answering, he bent her over his arm. Her back arched, her hair swung, the world went topsy-turvy and then he was lifting her to a stand.

"Now wave to the crowd," he said out of the side of

his mouth. "Maybe blow a couple kisses for good measure."

She waved and blew kisses, ignoring the flushed heat on her face, trying to imitate a figure skater after a medal-winning performance. The man with the sorcerer's eyes did a theatrical bow.

In that moment, Tiffany realized she'd found what she was looking for. That mythical creature she'd spoken of to Susie.

A good-time guy.

Tell him, she implored herself when he turned back to her. *Tell him you're in the market for a fling with a good-time guy.*

He put a large, warm hand on her shoulder and moved her out of the sight line of the gathered crowd, which was now listening to a jazzy rendition of "Danny Boy."

"What now?" he asked, providing her with the perfect opportunity.

She opened her mouth and took a deep breath to fortify herself with oxygen in order to get the words out, but still her voice trembled.

"I'm looking to have a good time," she said. "You interested?"

3

SHE HAD TO BE JOKING.

Chance had always believed the only place beautiful women propositioned strangers was in the Letters To The Editor section of men's magazines, and everyone knew those were made up.

And there was no mistaking that this woman was a beauty.

Model tall with long, silky brown hair, she was both slim and curvaceous. She had a long nose and a strong chin that bordered on square features adding character to a face that might otherwise have been too beautiful. Her dark lashes were decadently long, her eyes an exquisite almond shape, her mouth baby-doll pretty.

Except she didn't look as though she were joking.

Her brown eyes looked serious and...wholesome. Which didn't compute. He'd never heard of a wholesome siren.

Or a siren who flushed like a schoolgirl.

"Oh, my gosh." She moved away from him and covered her mouth with the fingers of both hands. "I can't believe I didn't figure this out before now."

"Figure what out?"

"You're married, aren't you?"

"I'm not married."

"Then engaged."

He shook his head. "Nope."

The hands dropped from her mouth. "Attached?"

He couldn't remember the last time he'd gone out with a woman more than once. It had probably been after law school when Ashley Ravenel hadn't understood why putting in extra hours at work were more important than spending time with her. After that, he'd kept his relationships casual, unwilling for another woman to claim he'd led her on.

"Not even remotely," he said.

Her eyes widened and that baby-doll mouth dropped open. "Then you're gay, aren't you?"

Amusement bubbled inside him, because she looked so darned...cute. That made her the rarest of creatures—a wholesome, blushing, cute siren.

"I wouldn't have kissed you like that if I were gay, now would I?" he asked.

She chewed on her plump bottom lip as she considered that, and he thought it amazing that moments ago his mouth had been on hers. If not for his pulse, which was reacting as though he'd just run a marathon, he'd have thought it had been a daydream.

"Then why haven't you answered?" she asked, reminding him of her question.

Did he want to have a good time? With her?

"Hell, yes," he said.

She smiled. "I knew it. I knew you were a good-time guy."

He, attorney Chauncy McMann, who'd carefully

crafted a legal reputation for himself in Atlanta before moving to the staid, storied D.C. law firm Whitaker, Baker and Taft, a good-time guy?

He clamped his jaw before his mouth gaped open. Neither the law partners who'd hired him nor the corporate clients he represented would share her opinion, but he tried to look at himself through her eyes.

She'd stumbled across him in a public square playing a borrowed sax and wearing a ludicrous shirt. He'd not only kissed her in full view of the gathering crowd but bent her back over his arm to acknowledge their applause.

No wonder she thought he was a wild man.

"About the shirt," he began.

"It's great," she interrupted. "If you were wearing neon, it couldn't have been a better sign that you weren't a Starched Suit."

"What's that?" he asked, although he knew it couldn't be anything good by the way her lips had curled.

"A man who spends so much time working he's ceased to exist outside of the suit."

Although Chance thought her definition harsh, he was fairly certain she'd have pinned the label on him before that bus had driven too close to the curb and splashed him with street crud.

But if he told her that some men in suits got great satisfaction from their work, he'd have to confess he wasn't the rebel she thought him to be.

What he was, he thought with sudden insight, was

a man who worked so much he didn't even have time to dwell on how little he played.

"I am sick to death of guys in suits," she said and rolled her pretty brown eyes. "Guys in suits do not know how to have a good time."

"I know how to have a good time," he said and hoped a lightning bolt from heaven didn't strike him down.

"Street musicians usually do."

Street musicians? This had gone too far. He'd already stretched the truth as much as he was willing. He couldn't let her believe a lie.

"I'm not a street musician. I'm a—"

When she placed two fingers against his lips, he had to restrain himself from flicking out his tongue to taste her.

"Shh. Don't tell me," she said. "I'd like some mystery in our relationship."

When she withdrew her fingers, he did his best not to grab them and put them back in place.

"We're going to have a relationship?" he asked.

"Relationship's probably the wrong word, considering I'm only in town for a visit." While she cast about for a more appropriate term, he almost moaned, noticing that she smelled like strawberries. He had a weakness for strawberries. "But I would like to have some fun."

So there it was again, the very strong hint that she was propositioning him. His pulse pounded at the thought of taking her up on the offer.

"Where to now?" she asked, flipping back her silky hair and exposing the long, lovely length of her neck.

Because he was a man without a hotel room, he hesitated. Because he was a gentleman, he wondered if it would be too bold to suggest they go to her place.

"I'm not much for drinking myself into a stupor," she continued, tapping her lower lip with a forefinger, "but Savannah's gone so crazy there must be something else we can do."

He stared at her in confusion. Despite that sizzling kiss and her request for a good time, she wasn't exactly suggesting they go off somewhere to have uninhibited sex.

"I want to do something wild," she said. "Something I've never done before."

Her eyes sparkled as she looked at him expectantly, as if he'd know exactly how to have a wild time. And why shouldn't she think that? He *was* passing himself off as a good-time guy.

"I know just the thing," he said to buy himself time to think of what that thing was.

His cabdriver had said that last year a man stripped to his skin and splashed in the dyed green water of a city fountain. As much as Chance wanted to see her naked, that was out.

"What is it?" she asked, her face bright with expectation.

As he desperately cast about for an idea, a red convertible backfired as it pulled up to the curb across the street. Four people got out of the car, laughing and talking loudly as they headed toward a house bright with lights and sounds.

"Let's crash that party."

Had that actually been his voice? Suggesting something he'd never done, not even while an undergrad at Duke. Then again, as captain of the crew team, he hadn't needed to be a party crasher. When he had time to unwind, which wasn't often, he'd been welcome anywhere he went.

She clasped her slim, long-fingered hands together. "That's a wonderful idea. I've never crashed a party before."

"It's a good time, I'll tell you that," he said and tried not to cringe.

But the plan to barge into a party uninvited was preferable to the alternative: Letting her go.

"Just let me get my bag," he said, walking over to the spot where he'd dropped it.

The suitcase the airline had lost was Louis Vuitton, but his leather carry-on was so worn it looked shabby. He saw her eyeing the bag and got ready to explain he'd bought it more than a decade ago with money he'd earned from a summer job working for a lawn-service company. It reminded him of the value of hard work, which is why he still carried it.

"I like your bag," she said, her eyes twinkling as though it pleased her that the good-time stranger she'd met on the street had a bag worthy of a vagabond.

The explanation died on his lips.

"Thanks," he said, coming over to stand next to her.

Magnolias bloomed in a colorful array behind her, but she had a simple beauty more appealing than the flowers. "Since we're crashing a party together, we should introduce ourselves."

"My name's Tiffany," she said. A pretty name that made him think of expensive jewelry and fine things. "What's yours?"

"Chance."

"Chance," she repeated and laughed. "Perfect. Because I'm in the mood to take one."

TIFFANY FELT HER FACE FLAME as they walked across the street toward the stately two-story gray-brick house where a party raged. They were so close she could feel the heat of his body.

She could hardly believe what she'd just said.

She'd meant she was feeling adventurous enough to take a chance on Chance. She hadn't meant she wanted to *take Chance.* That sounded as though she longed to drag him off to bed and have her way with him.

Not that the idea didn't have its appeal.

Chance was incredibly appealing, even in that kelly-green T-shirt. She couldn't imagine any of the men she associated with in D.C. ever wearing such a thing.

Then again, Chance wasn't like the men she knew.

Not only was he a self-professed good-time guy, but he wasn't out for everything he could get, like the self-serving politicians and lawyers she came into contact with daily.

If he had been, he'd have suggested something vastly different than crashing a party.

He'd have suggested something sexual, possibly involving silk sheets, slick bodies and scorching pleasures.

By landing that kiss on him even before she knew his name, she'd certainly invited that kind of proposition. After saying she wanted to take a Chance, she'd practically begged for it.

It was a wonder he hadn't pounced on her. Not that she wanted him to. She put a hand to her suddenly damp forehead. Not really.

She cast a sidelong glance at him and her breath caught. His nose had a slight bump, which made his profile seem more masculine. She loved a man with a strong chin and his was powerfully prominent. She didn't truly believe a strong chin portended a good character, but she thought it was true in Chance's case.

He turned, caught her staring at him and gave her a good-time grin. Her heart flip-flopped.

Okay. So maybe she wouldn't object if he did pounce on her.

"Ready?" he asked, and it took her a full three seconds to realize he was asking if she was ready to party crash instead of whether she was ready for him.

They were at the foot of the sidewalk, a step away from the wrought-iron rails lining a masonry stairway that led to a spacious porch and an entry door that was standing wide. Music poured out of arched windows that had been cracked open.

Was she ready to crash a party?

She didn't think so.

"Come on," he said, grabbing her hand and pulling her along as though he did this kind of thing all the time.

Her hand felt so good in his that it didn't occur to her to protest until they were already inside the house. Then it was too late.

The pale-pink walls of the entranceway stretched the full three stories of the house, bracketing a beautiful curved staircase. The hardwood floor was polished to a high shine and an elaborate crystal chandelier hung from the ceiling.

People were everywhere, milling in the hall, sitting on the stairs, spilling into the rooms.

None of them were much older than twenty.

"I think Mom and Dad are away and the kids have come out to play," she said close enough to Chance's ear that he could hear her above the rap song that seemed to make the very walls reverberate.

When the music suddenly stopped, the silence was almost eerie.

"Hey, man." A teenager in a lime-colored tank top with suspicion on his face and green streaks painted in his blond hair walked up to them. "What are you two doing here?"

Made, Tiffany thought. *They were made.* She tugged on Chance's hand to signal him that the gig was up.

"Hey, how you doing, buddy," Chance told the teenager, ignoring the hand tug. "Thanks for the invite."

The teen's brows drew together. Chance was probably closing in on thirty, which made him nearly ten years older than most of the guests. Surely the kid could tell they didn't belong.

Her stomach fluttered nervously, and she gave Chance's hand another jerk.

"I invited you?" the teen asked.

"We'd have been here earlier but we got caught up on River Street." Chance gave the kid a friendly slap on the back. "You know how that goes."

"Well, yeah, sure, but—"

"This is Tiffany," Chance said, ushering her forward with a hand at the small of her back.

The good manners that had been drilled into her since childhood kicked in and she automatically offered her hand. "It's a pleasure to meet you."

The kid took her hand, offering a weak shake. "Robert Thibodeau," he supplied.

"Rip to his friends," Chance added.

The kid gave him a penetrating look. "Nobody's called me that in a long time, man."

"I've known you for a long time," Chance said.

Confusion descended over poor Rip like morning dew on a magnolia blossom, but he did his best to mask it. "What's that nickname you use again?" he asked Chance.

"Chance."

"Yeah, that's it." The teen's laugh sounded forced. "The keg's in the kitchen. Go get yourself and your girl a beer, Chance."

"Will do." Chance pointed both index fingers at him. "Catch you later."

"That was amazing," Tiffany said when they were cradling mugs of green beer in a spacious, sparkling kitchen with little of the historical significance of the rest of the house. "But how did you know his nickname was Rip?"

Chance waggled his eyebrows. "Telepathy."

"You can read minds?" she asked dubiously.

"Not half as well as I can read the signature on the framed drawing of a clown his parents had on the wall," Chance said. "Rip probably drew it when he was a little guy."

"So that's how party crashers do it," she said, laughing. "They get in on pure chutzpah."

"If you let them see you sweat, it's all over," he said as a young woman in a sequined tube top and barely there green shorts shimmied by them. Within moments, five or six other people were dancing along with her.

"Shall we?" Chance asked, putting his beer mug down on a nearby counter and taking her drink.

"I can't dance in these shoes," Tiffany said, pointing to the stylish sandals that had gotten more uncomfortable as the evening wore on.

"Then take them off."

She couldn't do that. It simply wasn't done in the circles in which she ran. But that, of course, was the point.

She'd approached Chance because she was in the market for a new experience. Fighting self-consciousness, she reached down and unstrapped her sandals, then tossed them in a corner of the room.

"Let's get it on," she said as though she used such language all the time. The self-consciousness that gripped her grew when Chance took both of her hands and led her to an open spot.

The song, another rap number, called for some sort of fast boogie. Tiffany should have known how to dance to it, but rap had never been her music of choice. Besides, too many people crowded the kitchen to provide space to maneuver.

"How are we going to dance to this?" she yelled.

He gave her a sexy grin and pulled on her hand until they were chest to chest.

"Anyway we want to," he said, his warm breath sending a cascade of shivers down her body.

She was about to tell him that nobody slow danced to rap when he lifted her arms and did a nifty twist that had them both spinning three-hundred-sixty degrees without breaking hand contact.

"You, go," the woman in the halter top yelled. She beckoned to the other people in the kitchen, who formed a tight circle around them.

For the second time that night, Tiffany found herself the object of unwanted attention.

"What now?" she asked him, trying to mask her panic.

"We dance," Chance said and gave her another turn.

Her head spun, but she didn't think it was from dizziness.

It was from the preposterous realization that she, Tiffany Albright, champion of dairy farmers, was dancing barefoot with a sexy man in a stranger's kitchen.

"Chance! Tiff!"

The voice that rang out belonged to Rip, the host whose party they'd crashed. He stood on one of the kitchen chairs with both arms raised.

"Way to go!"

SHE WAS WILD WOMAN. Hear her roar.

The statements ran through Tiffany's mind as she walked through the Savannah night with Chance, but she didn't dare follow through on the roar.

Savannah had finally gone to sleep for the night. Aside from her and Chance, only the nocturnal birds that sang out from the majestic oaks seemed to be awake.

"You've got to be the best dancer I've ever been with," she told him, neglecting to mention she hadn't had that many partners.

"That's because you've never danced with my brother. With the possible exception of the moon-walking, he could put Michael Jackson to shame."

"What is he? A professional?"

"Not likely," he said, white teeth flashing in the night. His leather bag was slung across his back and atop his head was the green beret the party host had insisted he wear. "He's a doctor. The dancing is a well-kept secret."

"Why?"

"Because it's not dignified. Our mother signed us up for lessons when we were teenagers so we'd know how to slow dance, but I don't think she counted on them teaching us any fast numbers."

He twirled a green lei around his index finger like a lasso. It swished through the night air, catching the glint of the moon and adding to the surreal feeling of the night.

He had a brother who was a doctor? Who'd have guessed it?

"I suppose, being a doctor, he's not as carefree as you are," she said.

The lei stopped twirling. "You think I'm carefree?"

"You sure looked that way when you were dancing in the kitchen."

He laughed, a low, rumbling sound that sped up her pulse rate, the way it had been racing all night.

"What can I say? The music lives in me," he deadpanned. "And, I might say, in you."

She hoped the night hid the blush she felt creeping onto her face. Now that they were away from the party, she could barely believe the way she'd flung off various items of her clothes as they danced the night away.

Along with her shoes, she'd shed her suit jacket and scarf. She wasn't entirely sure, but she thought she'd been wearing a watch earlier in the evening, too.

And her hair...she reached up to touch it. Why had she let Chance and Rip convince her that it would look good spray-painted green?

"What time do you think it is?" she asked in a quiet voice.

He shrugged. "Two, three o'clock. Something like that."

She made a noncommittal sound, as though she wasn't the least bit freaked out about walking through Savannah in the wee hours with a good-time stranger.

Maybe she'd been wrong to cut him off earlier that night when he would have told her about himself. Already she wanted to know how a wanderer like him had ended up with a doctor for a brother. But every time she met a man who even remotely interested her, her parents did a background check.

She was sick to death of knowing everything there was to know about a man before learning the things that counted. So this time, she intended to fly blind.

Take that, doubting Susie, she thought. *I can too be unconventional.*

She stumbled over a crack in the sidewalk and he instantly took her arm. The shivery sensation she got whenever he touched her was back, along with her bold plan to have a fling with a wild man.

"Susie's place is around the corner," she said, hoping he didn't notice the catch in her voice.

"She's the friend you called earlier to tell her not to worry, right?"

"Right," she said, impressed that he remembered.

For a wild man, he had impeccable manners. He held doors open, said all the right things and was unfailingly polite. He was also a gentleman, darn it. This whole blasted plan would be that much easier if he weren't.

"It's that white Victorian with the arched black windows," she said when Susie's house came into view.

"We should be quiet so we don't wake her," Chance said as though he fully expected to deposit her at the front door and walk away.

"I'm staying at the carriage house around back," she clarified. "Susie rents it out, but she's between tenants. She's so busy with festival stuff she didn't want to wake me when she came home late."

She didn't add that Susie had no reason to suspect Tiffany would be the night owl. Her friend never phoned after eleven o'clock because she knew Tiffany would already be asleep.

"Yep, it's only me back there," she continued. "All by myself."

Great, she thought to herself in disgust. *The only way I could be more obvious was if I waved a neon sign in his face that said, Do Me.*

"Where are you staying?" she asked to make conversation.

He looked taken aback, as though he hadn't thought about it. "On a bench in the park, I guess."

"You don't have a hotel room?"

"All the hotels are full."

She stared at him, trying to understand what kind of man came to Savannah during the busiest weekend of the year without a hotel reservation?

A vagabond, she answered herself. An unconventional man.

4

HAD THAT BEEN A PROPOSITION? Chance wondered.

What was it about Tiffany that made it difficult to tell? And why didn't he haul her into his arms and find out exactly what her intentions were?

His reluctance surely wasn't because of a lack of attraction. He'd been aware of her every move all night. Hell, when they'd been dancing, he'd been *too* aware of her. He'd had to stop himself from dragging her into the nearest dark corner.

But now, as he walked with her down the skinny gravel road leading to the quaint little brick carriage house, she seemed...shy.

He frowned as he mentally added the adjective to the others he'd come up with. So now she was a wholesome, blushing, cute, *shy* siren.

"You're staying, aren't you?" She slanted him a look from under her decadently thick lashes. "I can't bear the thought of you sleeping somewhere on a bench."

Chance started to ask whether his staying the night would be okay with her friend when he stopped short.

He was supposed to be a good-time guy.

Good-time guys did not worry about permission

from the property owner when a beautiful woman asked them to spend the night.

Hell, a true good-time guy wouldn't have thought of the question.

"Show me the bedroom," he said so enthusiastically he thought he saw alarm leap in her eyes. If he wasn't careful, she'd show him the door before he got through it.

"I'm surprised you didn't make a hotel reservation," she said as she unlocked the door.

"I never do," he said truthfully enough. The law-firm secretaries usually handled the arrangements through firm-approved travel agencies.

But when Jake Greeley insisted his daughter's predicament be kept quiet, Chance had used an independent agent to book his Savannah trip. Who would have guessed her incompetence would turn out to be his gain?

"I always make reservations," Tiffany said as they entered the house. "I need to know I have a place to sleep."

So did Chance, but until a few hours ago he thought it would be in his own bed in his pricey apartment.

The plane that should have taken him back to D.C. had probably taken off at about the time Rip spray painted his hair green. The dye was supposed to wash out after a couple of washings, but he'd peered into a bathroom mirror and hardly recognized himself.

Now that they were inside the house, Tiffany seemed unsure of what to do. She ran one of her hands through her hair, which was as streaked with green as his own.

A huge brick fireplace dominated what was essentially one large room consisting of a compact living area, an alcove with a small table and a kitchen. A stairway led to the second floor and, Chance assumed, a bedroom and bath.

"I'm going to have a glass of water." She moved toward the kitchen while he dropped his beat-up bag beside the sofa. "Is there anything you'd like?"

Her eyes touched his and he felt the electricity that had been humming between them all night take hold and hang on. The single light she'd switched on wasn't enough to banish all the shadows, lending the room an intimate air.

"I do see something I like," he answered, holding her gaze.

He took a step toward her and she froze, seeming to forget all about that water she'd been about to drink.

She'd put her suit jacket back on for the walk from the party, and her chest rose and fell unevenly underneath the green fabric.

He wished she'd strip down to the stretchy sleeveless shirt that outlined the curve of her breasts and showed off her toned arms. Hell, while he was wishing, he might as well go for broke and wish she'd take off the shirt, too.

Her tongue darted out to wet her lower lip in a gesture he already knew meant she was nervous. The gentleman inside him wanted to hesitate, but he was supposed to be a good-time guy so he kept advancing.

When he was close enough to touch her, a pulse jumped in her throat. He reached out to stroke first the pulse point and then the soft skin of her cheek. Even his fingertips felt sensitized.

He was about to dip his head and kiss her when she blurted out, "You've got to admit that what you see is pretty great."

She was speaking at a clip easily twice her normal speed and the pulse in her throat was leaping again. He leaned back slightly to get a better view of her face. With her olive skin and exaggerated features, it *was* a pretty great face. He'd probably never tire of looking at it.

"That's what I was saying." His gaze dipped to her long, lean body which had more curves than angles. From what was visible to the naked eye, she was utterly perfect.

"I especially like the Whistle Walk," she added.

He narrowed his eyes, trying to process the information. He was familiar with Lauren Bacall, Humphrey Bogart and that famous scene when she told him to put his lips together and blow when he wanted her.

Was this Whistle Walk some variation of that? Did Tiffany mean she could whistle while she walked? And why did she think that was sexy?

"What are you talking about?"

"The covered walkway linking this house to the main one. In the plantation days, the servants had to whistle when they brought the food across so they wouldn't eat any of it."

"You lost me somewhere," he said, shaking his head. "Why are we talking about whistling servants?"

"Because historical significance is one of the things that make this house so great." Her eyes touched on his lips so briefly he couldn't be sure it happened. "You did say you liked it."

He'd said he liked *her*, a comment that shouldn't have been open to misunderstanding.

"Susie lived here until a few years ago when her mother died." Tiffany's conversation still came in rapid-fire spurts. "Even though she moved to the main house, she still loves this place."

"Will she mind if I spend the night?"

He nearly groaned before the words were out. He'd told himself, not fifteen minutes ago, that the good-time guy he was pretending to be wouldn't ask that question.

"Oh, no," she said quickly. "Susie always says what's hers is mine. She won't mind if you spend the night, but she might mind if you spend the night with..."

She stopped suddenly, but it wasn't too difficult to fill in the missing word. She meant Susie would mind if he spent the night with Tiffany.

"You're a grown woman," he said. "You shouldn't let anybody tell you how to live."

"I know that, and Susie does, too." She sighed. "But she's one of those people who worries about the people she cares about. Although I never could figure out why she thinks she has to worry about me."

Her eyes went dewy and again she seemed to focus on his mouth. Every muscle in his body tensed as he fought with himself not to reach for her.

"I know exactly what I'm doing," she said in a husky voice.

Chance didn't think so. If she did, she wouldn't be sending such mixed messages. One moment, she was a gorgeous temptress who seemed to want to hop into bed with him. The next, she was a mass of nerves.

Tiffany whatever-her-last-name-was clearly didn't know what she was doing. Or what she wanted.

The situation was clearer for Chance. What he wanted was exactly what he couldn't have.

He framed her face with his hands, steeled himself against the sexy little gasp she made and kissed her softly on the mouth. His lips wanted to linger but he wouldn't let them, not even when her hands clutched the material at the front of his T-shirt.

"Does Susie whistle when she comes down the walk?" he asked softly, his hands on either side of her flushed face.

She blinked once, then twice and the indentation between her brows grew pronounced. "If she did, they'd have to change the name to Wheeze Walk. That's what her whistle sounds like."

Even as he smiled at her comment, he wondered if he had completely lost his mind because of what he was about to suggest.

"Then I should sleep on the sofa. We wouldn't want to give your wheezing friend a reason to worry about you."

In the end, she simply unclenched her fingers from his shirtfront and nodded.

Later that restless night, Chance tried in vain to get comfortable on a worn sofa that had a terrific view of the interior of a fireplace that didn't blaze.

He might as well give up on sleep, turn on a light and review his notes on the case that had brought him to Savannah. If he'd spent tonight at that classy inn on River Street, that's what he would have done.

He anchored an elbow on the cushion and hoisted himself up halfway, but his thoughts drifted to the enticing woman sleeping a floor above him.

Was she naked? he wondered. If he crept up the stairs and slipped into bed with her, would their lovemaking fulfill the promise of those scalding kisses they'd shared?

His body stirred but then he remembered the indecision that had been written on her face as clearly as if someone had taken a pen to her skin. Linking his hands behind his neck, he lay back down and resigned himself to staying exactly where he was.

With his concentration so wholly focused on Tiffany, trying to work would be a waste of time. He sighed. He couldn't put off his legal obligations for long, but neither could he fulfill them any time soon. Not when he'd already canceled tomorrow's meetings.

What would it hurt, he thought, to concentrate on pleasure instead of business for the next few days?

Pleasure? Chance punched the lumpy sofa cushion

in frustration. He'd pretty much assured he wouldn't have any of that when he said he'd sleep on the couch.

Some good-time guy he was.

TIFFANY GROPED FOR THE PHONE at the side of the bed, wondering who could be calling at the ungodly hour of—she opened one eye—nine o'clock.

"'Lo," she said, not bothering to disguise the fact that finally, after tossing and turning most of the night with restless dreams, she'd been heavily asleep.

"Oh, good, you're awake." Susie's voice sounded as fresh as the spring flowers that adorned the city. "Did you have a good time last night?"

Tiffany sat up straight in bed, pushing errant strands of dark hair back from her face. "Is that a subtle way of asking if I went through with my fling?"

"Not really. Because, when I thought about it, I realized I was worried for nothing." Susie let out a short laugh. "I mean, you, pick up a man? I don't think so."

"Are you always this much fun in the morning?"

"Yes," Susie said brightly. "But you'll have to live without me this morning and the rest of the afternoon. That's why I called. To tell you I'll be gone until late working on parade stuff."

"If you're so sure I'm not with a man, why didn't you walk over here to tell me that?"

"I confided in Kyle about the way you were acting last night and he said I couldn't pop in unannounced. He said I wouldn't want to embarrass anyone, least of all myself."

"Then you should thank God for Kyle."

"I do, honey," Susie said, "every day I take a breath."

"Don't you want to know why I said you should thank God for Kyle?"

"Because he's as sweet as sugar and twice as tasty," Susie said without missing a beat.

"I'm very happy for you if that's true, but that's not it," Tiffany said. "I meant you should thank God for Kyle because I do have a man over here."

"A man? In your bed?" Susie, darn it, sounded downright disbelieving.

"Well, no," Tiffany said, cursing herself for not being able to lie. "He's downstairs on the sofa."

Susie laughed, a tinkling sound that grated on Tiffany's nerves. "Oh, honey, I don't know why I worry about you so much."

"What's that supposed to mean?"

"You can't even make up a juicy story."

"I'm not making it up!"

"Okay, whatever you say," Susie said. "But if you met a man last night and he's sleeping on the sofa, your idea of a wild time doesn't mesh with the rest of the world's."

TWENTY MINUTES LATER, her hair wet from the shower and thankfully no longer green, Tiffany was still fuming when she tiptoed down the stairs.

How dare disbelieving Susie imply that she didn't know how to have a good time. She'd not only approached Chance last night and laid a sizzler of a kiss on him but she'd brought him home with her, hadn't she?

And this morning, by God, she'd do more than kiss his beautiful mouth. She might be an accused conservative girl, but she was going to seduce the man on her sofa.

Her heart pounded so loudly that for a moment she thought she heard drums. Her blood rushed through her veins with the power of a broken dam.

She stopped at the foot of the stairs, drinking in the incredible sight of the sleeping man sprawled on her sofa.

And, oh my, he was an incredible sight.

The sun filtered through a partially open blind, casting a shadow where his thick lashes lay against his cheek. The strong angles of his face were relaxed in sleep, as though he'd given himself up to the power of it, and dark stubble had formed on his cheeks and jaw.

The flowered bedsheets were twisted at his waist, hinting at the restless night he must have spent and accentuating his potent masculinity. He slept on his back, one muscular arm flung over his head. His chest—oh, God, his chest—was bare.

He had the narrow waist and powerful shoulders of an athlete, with upper arms so well defined she wondered if he lifted weights. Taut skin lightly dusted with dark hair stretched over a network of ribs and muscles that would cause a sculptor to drool.

Tiffany wiped at her own mouth, surprised when she didn't encounter any moisture. He was so darned beautiful she yearned to reach out and stroke him. She wanted to rub her face against the stubble on his. She wanted him to wake up and provide a more satisfactory ending to the dreams that had left her aching and unfulfilled.

She wondered if he was naked under the sheet. She wondered what he'd do if she leaned over and kissed his sleeping mouth. She wondered why he'd stopped last night when she'd been able to tell at a glance that his body had been primed for her.

She must have walked over to the sofa, because she found herself standing there, one of her hands hovering above his body. She watched the even rise and fall of his chest and was close enough to feel the warmth of his breath when he exhaled.

Her breath caught at the realization of how much she wanted to touch him. She bent at the waist, her hand hovering above his chest, so near she could feel the heat his skin gave off.

She was going to do this. She was.

Except if she couldn't.

"Hey, there." His voice was husky with sleep. She snatched her hand back and straightened her spine so that she was once again standing over him.

Finally her eyes met his. Blue-green. Like the color of the sea when the sun was especially bright. His hair still held traces of green dye but amazingly that didn't detract from his potent appeal. Neither did the shadow of dark whiskers covering the lower part of his face.

Nope. This bare-chested, green-haired, whisker-intensive hunk was still the most enticing man she'd ever seen.

"Good morning." She risked a glance at the fireplace, wondering if it was possible to climb up it and disappear. "I hope you slept well."

"It's okay, you know," he said.

"I'm glad. Some people really hate to sleep on the sofa. They can't stretch out. Or turn over without feeling like they're going to fall off."

A corner of that sexy mouth lifted. "I meant it's okay if you touch me."

Her breath caught and her heart thudded. "What makes you think I want to touch you?"

"Besides the way your hand was hovering over my chest?"

She swallowed. "You saw that?"

He nodded, reached out and took the hand nearest the sofa. His thumb drew lazy circles into her palm and her throat went dry.

"I have a confession to make," he said, his voice no louder than a whisper. "I want to touch you, too."

Dear heaven, she thought as her knees went weak, where was a wall to lean against when you needed one?

She expected him to tug her down on the sofa beside him, but instead he released her hand. She nearly cried out at the lost connection.

"Why did you let go of my hand?" she asked.

He propped himself up on one elbow so that he was half sitting, half lying on the sofa. The gloriously defined muscles in his arm bunched. "Because I was making you uncomfortable."

The declaration was so stunning that Tiffany sat down in the small space between his body and the end of the sofa cushion. "Can I ask you something?"

"Anything."

She wet her lips and took a breath for courage. "Why did you stop last night?"

"Because you weren't sure."

Her heart melted like butter inside a hot skillet. He was right. Last night, she hadn't been sure she wanted to go to bed with him. They'd gotten inside the carriage house and the reality that she had brought home a wild, green-haired hunk had sunk in with a vengeance.

Most likely, if he'd tried to make love to her last night, she'd have stopped him, possibly even sent him on his way.

But he hadn't, which made all the difference in the world.

She reached out and ran her fingers over the scratchy surface of his jaw. His eyes widened with an unspoken question.

"I'm sure now," she answered and leaned over to kiss him.

She'd sampled his mouth before but this morning's kiss was softer, sweeter, gentler. He let her take the lead and she kissed one side of his mouth, the center, the other side. She ran her tongue over his lower lip, then his upper one. He groaned, but still didn't try to deepen the kiss.

She lifted her head and stared at him, dazed both by the passion heating her blood and the banked control in his eyes.

"This really is up to me, isn't it?" she whispered.

He smoothed her hair back from her face and nodded. "Entirely up to you."

"Amazing," Tiffany said.

The word applied to his body, her response to him, even the way they'd met.

But the most amazing thing of all was that no other man had ever given her the lead. All the other men who had been in her life simply assumed she wanted to be touched and wanted to be kissed because they wanted to touch and kiss her. Those men were so supremely sure of themselves they hadn't understood why she'd ultimately rebuffed them all.

That this man, of all men, should understand what she secretly craved was nothing short of a miracle.

A green-haired, sexy son-of-a-gun of a miracle.

She placed a hand on his breastbone and ran her palm over the warm, hair-roughened skin of his chest. The combination of hard muscle covered by warm skin made her pulse skitter.

"You were right," she said, feeling a little thrill at the way his breath came in shallow gasps. "Before you opened your eyes, I was coveting your chest."

Made bold by her own words, Tiffany lowered her head and licked first one male nipple, then the other. She wasn't sure what gave her more pleasure. The way the nipples hardened into nubs. Or his indrawn gasps.

"Tiffany," he said on a groan. "You're killing me."

"I can't have that," she said, stretching out on the sofa so she was lying flush against him. "I need you very much alive."

She felt the rumble of his laugh against her own chest before he said, "I've never felt more alive in my life."

She cut off anything else he might have said with a searing, mouth-open, tongues-mating kiss.

Her fingers spiked into his hair, cradling his head to allow greater access to his glorious mouth. Who could have known that this man's combination of lips, teeth and tongue would be so extraordinary?

By the time he moved his mouth to the hollow of her throat and nuzzled, they both were breathing raggedly.

"I sure hope I'm reading the signals right and yours are saying go," he rasped against her throat, "because this holding back is getting to be too much for me."

Tiffany boldly ran a hand down the center of his breastbone, past his flat stomach and under the bedsheet. She had her answer about whether he slept naked. He didn't. He was wearing the sweatpants he'd had on last night. That didn't stop her from rubbing the hard length of him through his clothes.

"Then don't hold back," she told him.

That was all the invitation he needed. Suddenly it felt as though his hands were everywhere, in her hair, caressing her back, stroking her legs, cupping her bottom.

She pressed against him, sex to sex, as he dipped his

head for a hard kiss, her pelvis moving restlessly against his. The only sounds in the room were the ticking of a clock, the hum of the refrigerator and their soft moans.

They were both wearing too many clothes. She wanted his sweatpants and underwear gone, her crop top and capri pants stripped away.

What had possessed her to dress like a tourist ready for a day of sight-seeing when she'd concocted the plan to come downstairs and seduce him anyway?

Could it possibly have been the hidden belief that she wouldn't be able to carry out the plan?

Every pore in her body seemed to be buzzing with sensation but still she laughed when she felt his hands on her cotton pants.

"What's funny?" he asked, drawing back to look at her. A faint smile touched lips turned red by her kisses.

"Me." Her confession came on a husky purr. "I'm not exactly dressed for seduction."

"I don't know," he said, getting a hand between their bodies and sliding it up her bare stomach until he was cupping one of her full breasts. "The crop top has definite advantages."

He frowned a little. "Although you could have done without the bra."

She caught her breath, so turned on that it was becoming increasingly difficult to talk. "It...unfastens...in the...front."

Within seconds, he'd unclasped the bra and her breast spilled free into his hand. He kneaded first one, then the other, drawing tight little finger circles around her nipples until they were hard and aching.

She pulled back from him abruptly and half sat on the sofa, yanking the top and the bra over her head in one quick motion before tossing them to the floor. He kicked back the sheets.

A streak of sunlight fell on his face, lighting up a killer smile that branded him ready for anything.

Like any good-time guy should be.

She felt a moment's fluttery panic but it disappeared the moment he pulled her back down and her bare chest was against his.

"You're so...beautiful," he rasped against her mouth before lowering his mouth to her naked breast.

She closed her eyes, savoring the feel of his hot mouth doing wicked, wonderful things to those intimate parts of her. Wanting more. Wanting him.

"I think..." she began just as he took her nipple into his mouth and nipped gently. She almost screamed in pleasure.

He raised his head and cocked a bad-boy eyebrow. "What do you think?"

"I think," she began again, knowing she'd had a point. He moved restlessly against her and she remembered what it was, "that we should get naked."

"Excellent suggestion," he said, lifting his hips and shucking his sweatpants and underwear so swiftly that she had to laugh.

"Your turn," he told her, but her hands shook so badly— From laughter? From nerve damage due to sensory overload?—that he had to help her.

He made as short work of her clothes as he had his own, and then they were naked. Gloriously naked. Their mouths locked and their bodies lined up so they were a perfect fit.

His hand glided down her body, creating sensuous little ripples wherever he touched, until he cupped her mound.

His tongue thrust into her mouth at the same time his fingers dipped into her heat. Her body stiffened, but then his clever fingers found her sensitive spot and she gave into the pleasure of being touched by him.

Wanting to give him something back, she cupped his erection, thrilled that he was already hard, hot and ready for her.

"Chance, now," she said when they broke off the kiss to surface for some much-needed oxygen.

She watched his face darken, his pupils dilate, the pulse in his neck throb and tried to prepare herself for what promised to be the most sensuous experience of her life.

"Aw, no," he said and put her away from him.

"Not what...you're supposed to say," she told him, her words coming in short bursts. She was more bewildered than hurt. "How about...sounds great...love to."

"I would love to," he said, his voice and face filled with urgency, "but I don't have a condom." Hope replaced the urgency. "Do you?"

She should, considering this seduction scene was her idea. She should have thought about birth control the moment she'd concocted the bright idea to hunt up a good-time guy. But she hadn't.

Some good-time girl she was.

"No," she said sadly and watched his hope die. She swallowed, still so turned on she probably could have generated enough electricity to heat the stove. "So that means we stop?"

Even to her ears, she sounded pitiful, like a child whose dessert—heck, whose main course—had been snatched out from under her nose.

"Oh, no, darlin'," Chance said an instant before his fingers started working their magic again. "I always finish what I start."

"But...but what about you?" she asked a moment before he transported her to a heated plane during which conversation was impossible.

"I'm not going anywhere," he drawled before she spilled her cries of release into his mouth.

5

WHAT IN THE NAME OF ALL things conservative did she think she was doing?

The surface answer was easy, Tiffany thought as she took a glance—a very long glance—at Chance whatever-his-last-name-was.

She was walking through the scenic, moss-draped heart of Savannah with a man who looked divine despite wearing the ridiculous tie-dye shirt and too-big shorts that had been left at the carriage house by a previous tenant.

It was the deeper answer that had her bordering on the throes of panic because the gorgeous man was a virtual stranger who was her soon-to-be lover.

"You're awfully quiet," Chance remarked.

Oh, gosh, even his voice was awe inspiring. Low and deep, the kind that seeped inside you and burrowed.

They were walking along roughly the same path they'd taken the night before. The sun beat down on Savannah, bathing it in light, but the day seemed no less mysterious than the night before.

She still didn't know what had gotten into her.

"I was wondering how we were getting to Tybee Island," she said, more or less truthfully.

She'd half expected him to disappear like the morning dew after their interlude on the sofa but instead he'd pointed out Savannah was in store for another unseasonably warm day and suggested they go to the beach.

But Tybee was fifteen or so miles east of the city, which seemed an impossible distance when neither of them had access to a car. Tour buses probably made the trip but somehow she couldn't imagine Chance inside one.

"It's a surprise," he said.

"You say that as if surprises are good things."

His brows, as gorgeous as the rest of him, lifted. "Aren't they?"

"If you think that, you must not find blind dates waiting for you at the table when you have dinner with your parents."

He laughed. "I avoid having dinner with my parents. My father's overly opinionated and my mother's—how can I put this?—judgmental."

"What does she do for a living?"

"She's a judge," he said and winked at her. His brother was a doctor and his mother was a judge? Before she could ask if he was serious, he asked, "What does yours do?"

"Finds boring bachelors and tries to fix me up with them." She frowned, not liking the picture of her life she was painting. She was supposed to be a good-time girl. "If only I could get her to realize I'm just a girl who wants to have fun."

I am, she told herself firmly.

Ha, a traitorous inner voice chimed in.

"My surprise'll be fun," he said. "I guarantee you that."

"Can't you give me a hint?" she asked, raising her voice to be heard above a dull roar that got louder with every step they took.

"I already have."

His sea-colored eyes sparkled, picking up the traces of green dye that hadn't entirely washed out of his luxurious dark-brown hair. He gave her a wink and took her hand. The contact was innocent, but the warmth of his skin made her remember the things they'd done on the sofa.

She and Chance hadn't been able to take their lovemaking to its natural conclusion but the experience still surpassed any that had come before it.

If just holding his hand made her skin heat, Tiffany thought she might spontaneously combust when they got around to the real thing.

Unless she let it sink in that she was contemplating these things with a virtual stranger and turned and ran.

At the thought of the things she was contemplating, she shivered.

"Don't tell me you're cold," he said, slanting her an amused look that had his eyes crinkling at the corners. "It's got to be eighty degrees."

Or at least that's what she thought he said because the dull roar had become a crescendo.

They rounded a corner and, through the low-hanging branches of a giant oak tree, she saw a half-dozen motorcycles gathered on the fringes of the historic square.

Big, black and powerful, the motorcycles appeared to be Harleys but their riders didn't seem like gang members. In their twenties, if that, the group of mostly young men resembled the crowd from last night's party.

Tiffany veered so as to swerve away from the place on the street where the cyclists had gathered, but Chance tugged her hand so they were walking toward it. Her ears vibrated.

"Hey, Chance, Tiff. Ready to go?" one of the riders called above the din.

Tiffany stopped short as it dawned on her why the cyclists resembled the group from last night.

It *was* the gang from the night before, with Rip on the lead cycle. He was dressed in jeans and a sleeveless black shirt that boasted a skull and crossbones, but he still looked preppy. Maybe because of the gel he'd used to make his hair stand up in trendy spikes.

"We're ready," Chance said, giving Rip a thumbs-up sign.

"Tiff, you ride with me." Rip jammed on his helmet and scooted forward on the cycle. "Chance, you can ride with Ashley."

Tiffany had a vague impression of Ashley as a slim blonde wearing tight faded blue jeans but Rip's motorcycle claimed the bulk of her attention.

Her pulse sped up and she took a step backward. Her preferred mode of transportation was a sleek, late-model car cooled not by the wind but by a delicately humming air-conditioning system.

How could she ride on that open-air aberration?

"Something wrong?" Chance asked when she didn't budge. He frowned. "Don't tell me you're not the kind of girl who rides motorcycles?"

The phrasing of his question reminded Tiffany of her conversation with Susie. What was it her friend had said? Oh, yes. That she wasn't the kind of girl who had affairs. Susie had implied that she was boring, that she didn't know how to have a good time.

She lifted her chin and gave an airy laugh.

"What could be wrong?" she asked and bravely went where she had never gone before.

THE WARM WIND IN CHANCE'S face felt glorious, but not as exhilarating as the feel of the powerful machine under his thighs.

Washington, D.C., and his life there seemed far away as he and the blonde sped down a man-made causeway lined with swaying palm trees and the tropical blooms of oleander and azaleas.

Why didn't he ride a motorcycle more often? he wondered as he raised his gaze to the blue sky and breathed in the scent of the salt marshes that bracketed the road.

Because he had more important things to do, he mentally answered himself. Things that involved legal settlements, courtrooms and billable hours.

Considering today was Friday and he typically didn't even take off weekends, this jaunt to the beach was a terrible extravagance. Guilt threatened to claim him, but then he remembered his vow to concentrate on pleasure. At least for today.

He let the wind sweep thoughts of the law from his mind as the blonde drove the hulking machine over a bridge and a road that cut a swath through a coastal marsh.

She dimmed the motorcycle's speed as they passed through the center of a city that oozed small-town charm. Soon they were heading down a strip of road adjacent to the beach where quaint inns, cottages and modest homes shared space with modern hotels and luxurious condominiums.

The sun that beat down on them seemed to seep through Chance's clothes and warm his soul. By the time the blonde pulled into a parking lot on the south end of the island beside a pier and pavilion, he was thoroughly relaxed.

Still he hesitated before getting off the bike, wondering when he'd find the time to take a spin on one again.

"Thanks for the ride," he told the blonde while he tried to remember her name. Ashley. Yeah, that was it.

"Don't mention it." She took off her helmet and shook out her long, blonde hair before giving him a come-hither smile. "I'd give you a ride anytime you like."

He pretended not to notice the invitation in her voice. Ashley was pretty in a sorority girl kind of way but that's what she was: a girl. Chance was interested in a woman.

He was saved from replying when Rip pulled up beside them with that woman wrapped around his waist like an octopus. The clamorous roar of the bike's motor had barely subsided when Rip let out a tremendous holler.

"That was way cool," he said, slapping the handlebars with one hand. He turned around, a grin bathing his young face. "Didn't you think it was cool, Tiff?"

"Oh, yes," she said as she peeled her arms from around him. "Great fun."

But her hands shook when she took off her helmet and she seemed unsteady when she got off the bike and joined Chance at the edge of the parking lot.

"Thanks, pal," Chance told Rip an instant before the boy revved the motor, gave the riders who had pulled into the parking lot behind him a hand signal and took off down the road.

"I can't believe they're just leaving us here alone," Tiffany said as they watched the motorcycles disappear into the distance.

Her eyes were wide in a face that had gone pale. A touch of what Chase thought was panic had entered her voice. Her brown hair, mussed from the helmet, was a wild tangle around her sweet face.

"There's no place I'd rather be than alone with you," Chance said, reaching out to smooth her hair. It was so silky, so soft.

"Really?"

The uncertainty in her voice made him realize that had sounded like a line. But he'd meant it. "Really," he said.

She swallowed and bit her lower lip. Her eyes didn't quite meet his as though she were...nervous? But that couldn't be. Not after what had happened the night before...and this morning.

He took his right hand out of her hair and trailed his index finger down her cheek. He loved touching her, would have loved it more if people hadn't been getting out of cars and gathering up fishing gear all around them. Then he could reach under her crop top like he had that morning.

"But..." She hesitated when his finger took a left turn and slid softly over her lower lip. He could feel a tremble but wasn't sure whether it was his finger or her lip. "...we still have a problem."

"What problem is that?"

"The problem of how we're getting back to Savannah."

The question effectively snapped the mood. Or maybe it was the step she took back from him. Or the bright sun beating overhead. Or the stream of cars pulling in and out of the parking lot.

He let his finger drop from her lip and forced himself to shrug, as though the question hadn't occurred to him. "We'll figure that out when the time comes."

"But—"

"Don't worry about it," he said, smoothing out the worry lines between her eyebrows. "If we run into Rip and his friends later, we can always hitch another ride."

She stiffened and her face seemed to turn even more pale. In dread?

"That was your first time on a motorcycle, wasn't it?" he guessed.

"A girl like me?" Her hand flew to her chest. The smile she gave him was brittle and overly bright. "The first time on a motorcycle? Oh, pu-lease."

She tossed her long, dark hair, which was still in a state of disarray. Like his thoughts. Why wouldn't she admit the obvious?

"Shall we go for a walk on the beach?" she asked.

Deciding it wasn't the time to quiz her, he let her change the subject. "I'd rather walk over to that restaurant," he said, nodding toward a handsome brick structure in the distance.

Surprise was clearly etched on her features. "Don't you want to grab some fast food and eat it on the beach?"

"Not when I can have one of Marmaduke's steak sandwiches instead." He shrugged. "What can I say? I'm addicted."

She gazed from him to the restaurant and too late he saw the establishment through her eyes. Huge glass windows affording diners a view of the beach bracketed the front of the eatery and an area was roped off for valet parking.

The place practically screamed expensive.

"You've eaten there before?" she asked.

"Not there specifically," he said. "Marmaduke's is a chain with restaurants across the South. I did some work for one of them."

She blew out a breath. "Oh, good. For a minute there, you had me worried."

"Worried about what?"

"Men who eat in restaurants like that," she said, gesturing toward the place, "wear suits."

He'd worn a suit when he worked there in his capacity as legal counsel for the owner of an Atlanta franchise who had been falsely accused of sexual harassment. He'd spent a week interviewing Marmaduke employees and another week convincing the plaintiff to drop the groundless charges.

"Tell me again what's wrong with men in suits," he said.

"Besides the workaholic, stuffy thing, you mean?"

He pressed his lips together. "You make men in suits sound like a mutant race. Like those things that live in the sewers in horror movies."

She laughed. "Only they bore you to death rather than scare you to death."

"So if I was wearing a suit last night, it would have killed my chances with you?"

He barely refrained from telling her his suits weren't flashy or trendy. He was into classic lines and traditional colors. There was absolutely nothing wrong with the suits he wore.

"Killed them dead. I might have noticed you but I wouldn't have approached you." She smiled at him. "I much prefer a waiter who plays the sax to a Starched Suit."

How had she jumped to the conclusion that he was a waiter? he wondered. And why was he finding it so hard to correct her misconception?

"I don't work at Marmaduke's," he began.

"I didn't think you did. Not anymore. You strike me as someone who gets around."

"I do?" he asked, then thought about his recent move from Atlanta to D.C. "I mean I do."

"I know." She smiled at him again, her brown eyes sparkling brightly in the afternoon sun. "That's one of the things I like about you. So how about that steak sandwich?"

He frowned and took her hand. "On second thought, why don't we pick up fast food? Seems I've lost my taste for steak."

And anything that might clue her in that he spent most of his life in a suit.

He closed his eyes briefly as they walked in the direction most likely to yield one of the popular places that specialized in hamburgers and fries, neither of which he ate with any regularity.

But if he told her that, he might as well admit he was a Starched Suit. And say goodbye to those smiles of hers that were becoming more addictive than oxygen.

"Come on," Chance invited in a voice so sensual and throaty it caused Tiffany's heart to race. "I'm waiting."

His wide, chiseled chest was bare, making him resemble some sort of irresistible sex god. He stretched out a long, muscular arm and beckoned to her with a crooked index finger.

"Come on," he repeated in his low-timbered voice. "Unless you're afraid."

"I'm not afraid," Tiffany managed to say, although she could barely hear herself over the wild beating of her heart. She took a step forward and a shiver ran from her toes to the top of her head.

"Oh, that water's freezing," she said as the remnants of an ocean wave lapped at her feet and, she imagined, turned them blue. "It can't be more than sixty-five degrees."

"Sixty degrees," Chance called from where he stood in the surf in waist-deep water. "That's what the guy in that beach shop told me."

He was referring to the shop where they'd bought a beach blanket and bathing suits, the better to enjoy the sun, the sand and the unexpected heat wave that had descended upon coastal Georgia.

She'd been a sport in the beach shop, going along with Chance's suggestion that she buy a cherry-red bikini briefer than anything she'd ever worn in public.

She'd convinced herself that she felt comfortable wearing next to nothing as she'd squished her bare toes in the sand while strolling the beach with Chance, munched on a cheeseburger and lounged on their oversize beach blanket.

Despite the way she'd closed her eyes the entire drive out to the beach and prayed God would deliver her from any more motorcycles, until a few minutes ago she'd believed she was brave enough to spend the day with a wild, sexy man.

"If he told you the water was that cold, why did you go in?" she asked as goose bumps popped up on her legs, arms and even her stomach.

"Because you only live once," he said and did a graceful dive under an approaching wave. He surfaced a moment later, shaking his hair back from his face so that droplets of water glistened against the sunlit blue sky. He laughed his pleasure, then turned those dancing eyes on her.

"Come on," he called again, once more stretching out his arm. "It's invigorating."

Tiffany braced herself so she wouldn't run back to the safety of the sunny beach, branding herself as a tame woman dressed in wild-woman clothing. After all, the water wasn't cold enough to cause frostbite. She didn't think.

She gulped in a lungful of sea air for courage, squared her shoulders and took a run on the wild side—directly into the frigid ocean water.

She didn't dare stop until she reached his extended arms, lest she turn right back around. He anchored his hands under her armpits and lifted her into the air, facing deeper water. He swung her around once, then twice, until they were both breathless with laughter.

Then he let her go.

She took a breath and held it while she was still airborne and then the ocean rose to meet her with an open, frosty palm. It took her into its icy depths, and she shot back up to the surface utterly soaked.

As her shiver turned violent, she wondered lamely if she'd be warmer had she gone with her gut and opted for a one-piece bathing suit.

"This is like jumping into a vat of ice cubes,"

she said as Chance swam a few powerful strokes to her side.

"It's not that bad," he said when he reached her. His lips weren't quite blue but they no longer looked red, either. Hers had probably transcended blue and turned a deep shade of purple. "There's a sandbar just beyond us, which is why the waves aren't big here. The water's warmer, too."

"Warm?" she said incredulously as her teeth began to chatter. "To...to a p...p...polar bear, maybe."

"I know a way to warm you up," he said and waited.

His meaning was clear from the sudden heat that flared in his eyes, as though he were standing in front of a fireplace instead of the waist-deep frigidness of the Atlantic.

But he didn't reach for her, the same way he hadn't pressed her to make love the night before.

He was leaving the decision up to her, she realized. Like a gentleman and unlike so many of the wolves in Starched Suit clothing she ran across.

Her breath caught, her heartbeat quickened and she forgot that she'd lost the feeling in her extremities.

"Th...th...then what are you waiting for?" she asked him.

His smile was wide and so sexy she would have swooned if she hadn't remembered in time that would mean taking a dunking. He reached for her at the same time she came forward. The entire cold length of her was now flush against his hard, wet body, leaving her no doubt about what he had in mind.

"I d...d...didn't think a man could get an..." She trailed off, too shy to specifically refer to the erection pressing against her, and tried again. "I mean, the water's so c...c...cold and, um, other parts of you feel c...c...cold, too."

He chuckled a little before the gleam in his eyes turned even hotter.

"When you're around, no way could I be cold for long," he said and kissed her.

For a moment her lips were so numb that she could barely feel his moving against them, but it was just a moment. Then pleasure hit her so intense she gasped from it. And just like that, his tongue was in her mouth, stroking and swirling and making it highly unlikely that her body would ice over.

A wave struck behind them, dousing them with spray, but the surf wasn't rough today and it barely made a ripple in the ocean surface. Still, Tiffany hooked one of her legs around Chance's to anchor herself to him. She dug her fingers into his wet, cold hair and kissed him back for all she was worth.

A thrill leaped through her when she felt the hard evidence of his desire against the juncture of her thighs, the same way it had the other times she'd kissed him. She didn't know how and she didn't know why but being in this man's arms was shockingly different than being held by anyone else.

The sensation was hotter, wilder, more electrifying. One of his hands skimmed her rib cage and came around to cup her breast. Her nipple was already hard from the cold but she felt it tighten nonetheless as a warm, liquid sensation flowed through her.

He moved his mouth from hers to the sensitive place on her neck just beneath her ear.

"Warmer?" he asked against her skin.

"I'm still shivering," she said as she tilted back her head to give him better access to her throat, "but I don't think it's from the cold anymore."

His laugh was deep and so sensual she couldn't have stopped herself from rubbing against him even if she wanted to.

And she didn't want to.

She might have resisted if he had taken what he wanted without asking but he'd left it up to her. And, oh, that was an incredible aphrodisiac.

When he removed the hand that was squeezing and teasing her breast, she gasped in protest. But then that hand was on her bottom, caressing her skin through the skimpy material of her bathing suit.

She made a soft sound of pleasure and reached between their bodies to stroke the hard length of him.

"Ah, Tiffany," he said above the roaring of the surf. "You don't know what you're doing to me."

But she did know. She could hear it in his shallow breathing, feel it in the rapid beating of his heart, in the way his body had hardened when she'd gone into his arms.

He wanted her, perhaps as much as she wanted him. Although that hardly seemed possible.

She wanted him here, now, buried deep inside her. She wanted it more than she'd ever wanted anything.

A humming filled her ears and for a moment she thought it was the rush of her own blood. But as it got louder she gradually realized it was the whir of an outboard motor.

She raised her head and spotted a motorboat in the distance. Another sound—was it laughter?—carried on the ocean breeze and she scanned the beach.

It wasn't crowded but she could see people in the distance, people who could look out into the ocean and figure out what she and Chance were doing.

"Chance," she breathed, "we have to—"

What she'd been about to say was lost when he moved his mouth over hers and kissed her again.

She'd forgotten about the cold minutes ago but now even the heat of his kiss couldn't chase it away. It was back with a vengeance because they couldn't do this. Not here. Not now.

With a tremendous burst of willpower, she wrenched her mouth from his. He looked at her with dazed, confused eyes.

"Chance," she repeated. "We can't."

His hands stilled on her bottom. He didn't try to kiss her again but she could tell that's what he wanted.

All she had to do was say the word and he'd make love to her here in the ocean. She was tempted because logically she knew the people on the beach were too far away to know for sure what they were doing, especially since she and Chance were in water above their waists.

But it was no use. No matter how much she wanted him—and oh, how she wanted him—she couldn't make love to him here.

"I can't," she repeated, anchoring her hands on the solid width of his shoulders.

She fought not to cry out in protest when he lifted his head and, with obvious reluctance, removed his hand from her bottom. His eyes were closed and she could see the whiteness around his mouth, the strain on his face.

"Of course you're right to stop us," he said, then opened his eyes to look at her. The blue-green of his irises nearly perfectly matched the color of the ocean water. "I still haven't picked up those condoms."

She stared back at him for a moment, stunned at his assumption that the lack of a condom was why she hadn't gone through with their lovemaking but even more dazed by the statement.

Because, for only the second time in her life, she'd forgotten about the necessity of birth control.

He took a step back from her and a wave broke nearby, sending a cold blast of water rushing over them.

"Let's get out of the ocean," he said, giving her a rueful smile. "You might not have noticed, but the water's freezing."

6

As the pickup truck barreled into Savannah with noisy gusto, Tiffany tried to stop her butt from bouncing against the ridged bed where she sat huddled inside the beach blanket.

It was no use.

Barump, barump, barump went her butt.

"Ow, ow, ow," she thought.

But she didn't complain aloud, just as she hadn't griped about the truck's blown-out muffler. Or the way she had to keep her head perfectly still. If she turned to one side, her hair whipped around her face like a dark curtain. But that was preferable to turning her head to the other side, where only severe teeth gritting prevented insects from flying into her mouth.

"Almost there," Chance said.

He sounded disappointed, as though he could have kept riding in the back of the pickup truck for another hundred miles. Despite the temperature dipping into the sixties, he hadn't even wanted to share what little warmth the beach blanket provided.

To be fair, he'd given her a chance to veto the offer of a ride when the trio of teenage boys had issued it.

But she hadn't had the heart or the body heat to say no.

Boy, had she been wrong.

"Here we are," Chance said cheerfully when the pickup truck came to a halt and the noise mercifully stopped. She had to grab on to him to prevent from toppling over. "How'd you like this for door-to-door service?"

She assumed they'd pulled up in front of Susie's house, although she couldn't tell for certain. She'd made the mistake of turning her head to try to get her bearings and her hair was in her eyes.

She swept it back and tried to smile but couldn't. She must have subconsciously gnashed her teeth to make absolutely sure she kept the bugs at bay and her jaw seemed to be locked in place.

She unclenched it and tried to think of something positive to say. Unfortunately all she could think of was, *Thank the Lord that's over.*

And she didn't think she should say that.

"Very good," she muttered.

In her experience as a lobbyist, it was the perfect phrase because it essentially meant nothing.

Chance anchored one hand on the side of the pickup bed and hopped out of the truck with athletic grace. Tiffany got up much more slowly, nearly tripping over the beach blanket in the process. She folded it the best she could and gingerly made her way to where Chance was standing, his arms outstretched to help her down to the street.

She went into his arms eagerly and only partly because Chance was the hottest guy she'd met in a long time.

She probably would have gone to Godzilla if it meant she didn't have to ride another mile in the infernal pickup.

The instant she was clear of the truck, the driver blared his horn and took off down the road, his ruined muffler making enough noise to raise the dead.

Chance waved his thanks.

"Tiffany?" The shocked, familiar voice startled Tiffany out of Chance's embrace. "Is that you?"

She forced herself to turn around slowly, exactly the way she would have if somebody had tapped her on the shoulder at a cocktail party. She schooled her features not to betray her prearoused state and the honeyed sensations that were still flowing through her.

"Oh, hello, Susie," she said to the stunned blonde who was gaping at her with her mouth open. Her boyfriend Kyle, who towered over Susie by a good foot and had his long hair pulled back from his strong, angular face, stood beside her. "Hello to you, too, Kyle."

"You just got out of a pickup truck," Susie said before Kyle could return the greeting.

"I'm sure Tiffany knows that, Suse," Kyle said mildly.

Susie seemed not to hear him. "And you're with—oh, my God—a man."

"I bet she knows that, too," Kyle said.

Tiffany cleared her throat. "Susie, Kyle, let me introduce you to Chance..." Her voice trailed off, a fact Susie instantly picked up on.

"You don't even know his last name!"

"It's McMann," Chance supplied, stepping forward to shake first Susie's, then Kyle's hand. "Chance McMann."

"You exist," Susie exclaimed.

Chance's laugh came out as a low rumble. His hair, stiffened by the salt water and tousled by the wind, was a delicious mess above his tanned face. With his unconventional clothing and long, hard limbs, he looked almost uncivilized.

"Last time I checked, that was true," Chance said. "I do exist."

Susie shook her head, mumbling half to herself, "I can't believe it. I didn't think you did, not even when I called Tiffany this morning and she said you did, but here you are."

"We were at the beach," Tiffany cut in before Susie's mutterings revealed the reason for her shock.

It wasn't hard to figure out. Deep down, Susie hadn't believed Tiffany had enough moxie to pick up a man. Or to hitchhike a ride in the back of a pickup truck. Or to make out in the surf.

"It was a good day for the beach," Kyle said when Susie opened her mouth to say something else. "The sun was hot."

Chance gave Tiffany a long, appreciative look that conveyed the sun wasn't the only thing he thought was hot.

"But the water was cold," Chance said, winking at her. "Ask Tiffany."

Susie actually gasped aloud. "Ask Tiffany?" she repeated. "You can't mean she actually went in the ocean."

"It was nice meeting you," Kyle said, taking Susie's arm and doing something with his eyebrows Tiffany interpreted as a signal for Susie to shut up. "But Suse and I have a concert we need to get to."

Kyle tugged, but Susie didn't move. Her blue eyes fastened on Tiffany. "But that's crazy. Nobody goes in the water in March."

Kyle tugged again but Susie still didn't budge. She'd planted her feet a shoulder's length apart and seemed to have settled in for the night.

"Suse, if we don't get going," Kyle urged, "the musicians won't know where to set up."

"But...but..." Susie sputtered.

"I'm fine, Susie," Tiffany said in a soft voice, stepping forward to put a hand on her friend's arm.

"How can you be fine?" Susie whispered back so only Tiffany could hear. "You're not acting like you."

Her eyes flicked to Chance before settling back on Tiffany. They were filled with such obvious concern that Tiffany tried to see Chance through her friend's perspective.

With his muscular upper body and long, ropy legs, he was undeniably sexy. The hypnotic eyes, little bump on the bridge of his nose and luxuriant thickness of his dark-brown hair lent him the kind of untamed good looks that could make a woman forget her good sense and embark on a wild affair.

The wrong kind of woman could end up getting scorched.

"I'm fine, Susie," Tiffany repeated, but she no longer sounded sure, not even to her own ears.

"You heard Tiffany, Suse, she's fine," Kyle said and looked relieved when Susie's feet finally unstuck from the sidewalk. Kyle quickly propelled her forward.

"Good to meet you," he called over his shoulder to Chance as he spirited Susie away, not once breaking stride.

Chance watched them go with a bemused look on his face.

"What was that all about?" he asked as they walked together past the main house along the driveway leading to the carriage house.

Tiffany forced herself to shrug. "I told you last night that Susie was overprotective."

His eyebrows rose. "You weren't exaggerating."

"Yeah, well, like I said before, I'm only visiting. I haven't seen her in a long time so she doesn't know me all that well anymore."

The implication being that if Susie had been better acquainted with her these days, she'd know Tiffany was more than equipped to handle a man like Chance.

Ha, that little voice inside her head said when Chance's hand brushed hers as he took the beach blanket so she could unlock the door.

How could she handle a man when his touch made desire wash over her like a wave?

"People change," Chance said, but Tiffany's hands shook when she tried to insert the key in the lock and she knew she hadn't.

She'd tried to fool herself into believing she was

brave enough to walk on the wild side but everything that had happened today proved otherwise.

She'd hated the motorcycle ride, barely tolerated the pickup and despaired at dunking so much as a toe in the frigid ocean water. Most tellingly, she hadn't the guts to make love to Chance in that water even though nobody had been within fifty feet of them.

Now that darkness had fallen and they were once again in Savannah, she doubted she had the nerve to make love to him in private either.

She was no more a good-time girl than a nun.

"Need any help with that key?"

She hadn't left on a porch light and his voice came out of the darkness behind her, low and as sultry as the night.

"No. I got it," she said, finally inserting the key in the lock on the third try.

He opened the door for her and she stepped into the house, turning on a light near the entrance. Her heart beat hard as she waited for the touch of his hands on her shoulder, waited for him to turn her around so they could finish what they'd started in the ocean.

Oh, Lord. Even though he was the sexiest man she'd ever met, she didn't think she could do this.

But instead of his hands, she felt...a soft, fluttery breeze.

She turned to see Chance standing on the doorstep, beyond the open door.

"Aren't you coming in?" she asked, tipping her head quizzically.

"You tell me," he said, still not moving. The interior

light cast him in a golden glow that illuminated his questioning expression. Behind him, the night was black and the air fragrant with the scent of spring blossoms.

"We were gone all day," he continued, "so I didn't get a chance to call hotels to see if any rooms had become available."

He was doing it again. Leaving the decision of how their relationship would proceed up to her. Standing back and giving her space, time to think. But it wasn't enough time. She needed more.

"If there weren't vacancies yesterday, do you really think there'd be any today?" she asked, stalling.

"I won't know unless I try."

She wet her lips, unsure of what she was going to say until the question escaped her lips. "Do you want to try?" she asked, and her voice sounded small.

He looked her straight in the eyes, holding her gaze as though in possession of a powerful magnet. Her breath caught in her throat. When her lungs felt starved for air, she forced herself to suck in some more oxygen.

"Hell, no," he said.

She felt herself smile, heard the little laugh of joy bubble from her lips. And just like that, she made her decision.

She'd bought a short, gauzy cover-up at the beach to wear over her string bikini, liking the way its pale yellow hue lent it a demure air.

But there was nothing demure about the way she slowly unfastened the row of buttons that ran down the center of the garment. Or the way she slipped it off her shoulders so she was wearing nothing but the bikini.

"Then what are you standing all the way over there for?" she asked in a voice so husky she hardly recognized it as her own.

For a moment, Chance could only stare at her in stunned disbelief.

Her body language had been screaming "back off" since she'd told him she couldn't make love in the surf. Not that it hadn't been the right decision. He'd been so out of his mind with wanting her it hadn't dawned on him that they didn't have birth control until it was almost too late.

He wasn't sure what had changed from then to now but he'd be blind, deaf and so very dumb to ignore what Tiffany's body language was telling him now.

He stepped into the house, kicked the door shut behind him and prepared to take her up on her invitation.

The merest flicker of what might have been doubt flashed across her face before he reached her but he'd already used up his supply of willpower.

"I hope you're sure," he said when his arms were around her and his lips were inches from hers, "because I don't think I can stop a second time."

"I don't want you to stop," she said, threading her arms around his neck and pressing herself against him from chest to groin.

He groaned and buried his face in the tender place

alongside her neck, just under her ear, barely able to believe she was letting him hold her nearly naked body in his arms.

He'd thought about little else but touching her since he'd talked her into buying the red bikini. She looked like a pin-up model in it. Her breasts were high and firm, her stomach flat, her legs long.

The incredible thing was that she didn't seem to know how truly spectacular she looked.

And that might have been the biggest turn-on of all.

"I've been wanting to do this all day," he said, running his hands over the smoothness of her back and cupping the firmness of her buttocks.

"You did do it." Her voice was breathless and he felt a surge of male pride that he was the cause. "In the ocean."

"Yeah," he said, chuckling a little, "but it doesn't feel the same when your hands are frozen."

"I thought you liked—" she gasped when he brought one of his hands up to stroke the side of her breast "—the cold."

He had. The chill had been exhilarating, heightening his senses so that every part of him had come screamingly alive.

He hadn't thought he could feel more alive—until Tiffany had come into the water with him.

"I do like the cold," he said, moving his mouth once again so that it hovered above her lips. "But I'll take the heat any day."

She stared at him for a moment and he saw that

heat in her eyes, turning the flecks in her brown eyes even more golden, like firelight.

Unable to wait any longer, he crushed his mouth down to hers, thrusting his tongue between her lips to part them. But her mouth was already open and welcoming and her tongue tangled with his in a slick, heated glide.

His hands came up to hold her head in place so he could gain better access as he deepened the kiss. She kissed him back, meeting his passion, adding her own.

He was already harder than he ever remembered being in his life, his erection so hot and heavy it was a wonder it didn't rip his shorts.

After a few more moments of mindless kissing, he reached around her back to undo her bathing suit strap. He fumbled with the tie for a moment in which she pressed her breasts against his chest and then he couldn't bother with it anymore.

He gave a tug and heard the fabric rip, but he didn't care. He didn't care about anything except baring her beautiful breasts and bringing his mouth down to feast, tasting the salt of the ocean on her skin, hearing her moan vibrate in his ear.

Out of control, he thought dimly. He was completely out of control, which had been the direction he'd been heading in the ocean before she drew back.

It was a direction he'd never before taken, not with any woman.

He'd prided himself, in fact, on being in control at

all times. He was a McMann and McManns lived their lives calmly, coolly, deliberately.

"Oh, Chance," she said so breathlessly it seemed as though she was out of control, too, "don't stop."

As if he could.

He reached inside her bathing suit bottom, found her center and slid two fingers inside her. She was slick and wet and cried out her pleasure.

At that moment, he found it very hard to care that he had no control where she was concerned.

He tried to strip off her bathing suit bottom and it ripped, too, but he felt no remorse for the ruined garment.

Not when Tiffany was naked and impatient. Not when her hand was alternately stroking him through his shorts and trying to tug off his clothes.

With difficulty, he stepped back from her and made short work of tearing off his shirt, shorts and briefs. He reached for her, and the feel of her naked skin against his made his blood heat.

He kissed her again, his mouth open and seeking, and one of her legs wrapped around his upper thigh as she pressed her most intimate part against him.

"The bedroom," she gasped when she turned her mouth away from his a moment later. "Shouldn't we go to the bedroom?"

Blood was roaring in his ears and he was hot and pulsing against her, but he managed somehow to nod. He even managed to reach down and pick up his shorts. One of the pockets had a supply of condoms that they'd bought in a drugstore before hitching a ride back to town.

Then he swept her into his arms and headed for the stairs leading to the bedroom. He might have gotten farther than the first step if she hadn't kissed him.

He kissed her back, the sensation wet and wild as he fondled her breasts. His legs felt unsteady and then he was sinking with her.

"We're on the stairs," she whispered when he was no longer supporting her and her fingers tangled in his hair.

He focused on their surroundings. She was right. They were on the stairs. But the bedroom seemed so very far away.

He flipped their positions so that his back was against the unyielding hardwood steps and then he drew her onto his lap so that her knees were on either side of his thighs and his erection nudged at her opening.

"Here," he rasped. "Now."

"Yes," she said, her eyes so dark with passion he could barely distinguish the pupils. "Oh, yes."

And then he was tearing open the foil packet and sheathing himself with fingers that fumbled. It seemed an eternity until he was protected.

"Now," she said, and he thrust upward at the same time as she lowered herself.

She was tight, so very tight, and slick. He closed his eyes, feeling beads of perspiration on his upper lip. He wanted to make this good for her but he was so turned on he was afraid he'd split apart if he moved.

But then she was the one who moved, lifting her hips so that he was partway out of her and then lowering herself to take the whole of him back inside her. Her head was thrown back, her skin flushed with passion. He thought she was the most beautiful woman he'd ever seen.

She anchored herself with both her hands on a step above him, and he watched her eyes glaze over as she lowered her hips once again. He couldn't help it. His hips began to move. And then he was out of control.

He slammed into her, and her cries of pleasure urged him to go faster and faster. The tension built with amazing speed so that Chance couldn't have slowed down even if she'd wanted him to. Still, he tried.

"Faster," she gasped, thrusting downward to take him more completely inside her.

It was enough. He felt her inner muscles contract around him, heard her shout and then he shattered in a burst so blinding and powerful that he shook from it. The shaking persisted, like the aftershocks of an earthquake, until dimly he realized he'd just had the best sex of his life.

She collapsed against him, breathing hard, her body as slick with sweat as his own.

He held her tight, trying to get his breathing under control while his rapid heartbeat gradually began to slow. It wasn't until she spoke that he became aware of the hardwood of the steps biting into his back.

"We didn't make it to the bedroom," she said.

He didn't come out of his haze until she lifted herself from him and off the steps, leaving him bereft.

He looked up at her, past the long legs and curly mound of hair, his gaze touching on the slight sexy pouch of her stomach and those gorgeous breasts before settling on her beautiful face. He'd kept his eyes open when she climaxed and thought he'd never forget the look of ecstasy he'd put on that face.

She gave him a tentative smile, as though unsure of what he was thinking. She was about to find out.

Getting to his feet, he hooked an arm behind her knees and swung her luscious naked body into his arms. He grinned down at her. "I can't guarantee we'll make it to the bedroom this time, either."

She giggled. He had it bad, he thought, when even her giggle was arousing.

He was already growing hard so he wasted no time in bending down to pick up his shorts with their cache of condoms. He headed for the bedroom with her in his arms, taking the steps two at a time as a matter of expediency.

It didn't help.

This time they only made it to the hallway outside the bedroom door.

IN THE MIDDLE OF THE NIGHT, Chance's right hand—the hand of her *lover*—cupped her left breast and began a slow journey down her naked stomach.

Pinpricks of sensation sprang up wherever he touched, sensations so sharp Tiffany was surprised anew.

This wasn't the first time he'd awakened her. They hadn't gone to sleep immediately when they'd finally gotten to the bed, either.

Tiffany hardly had time to be shocked at the way they'd made love on the steps and then against the wall in the hallway before he'd filled her again, the way he was making it clear he wanted to fill her now. She sighed into his mouth when he rolled over and kissed her.

She could feel the swirl of hair on his chest as he pulled her against him, the hard muscles of the legs that were tangled with hers, the heat of his erection.

He broke off the kiss and buried his face in the crook of her neck, laughing a little. "I can't seem to get enough of you," he said, sounding breathless.

She could have echoed the sentiment.

She'd half convinced herself she wasn't cut out to walk on the wild side until that moment downstairs when she'd stripped off her cover-up and offered herself to him like an experienced temptress.

That couldn't have been a fluke, not when she wanted Chance to make love to her over and over again.

So what if she didn't know which section of the newspaper he read first? If he liked orange or cranberry juice better? Whether he preferred Bugs Bunny or Peter Rabbit?

So what if she wouldn't even know his last name if Susie hadn't pointed out that she didn't? So what if he still didn't know hers?

"It's Albright," she blurted out.

His head lifted. Her night vision had adjusted and she could read the question in his eyes. "Excuse me?"

"My last name. It's Albright," she said, then swallowed. Why had she told him that? "In case you were wondering who you were in bed with."

He tenderly skimmed the backs of his knuckles across her cheek. "Oh, I know who I'm in bed with."

He brought his hand back to her breast to knead and tease. He drew a circle with his forefinger on the nipple and it instantly tightened.

"I'm in bed with a beautiful, sensuous woman who I can't stop touching," he said as he continued to play with her breasts. He nuzzled the side of her neck, then kissed her lips, quick and hot. Her body gave a sensuous shiver.

"Really?" she asked as a band seemed to tighten around her heart. "Not knowing anything about me isn't a problem for you?"

She could have bit her tongue for asking because of course it wasn't a problem. He wasn't like her. He'd probably been on a first-name-only basis with plenty of his lovers.

"Who says I don't know anything about you," he said, bringing his hand down to part her legs.

"I know you like it when I do this," he said as his fingers found her moist center and she cried out.

He kissed her, swirling his tongue inside her mouth. "And that," he said, grinning at her when he raised his head.

He reached onto the bedside table, ripped open a

packet and quickly covered himself. She helped guide him into her, sighing with pleasure.

"And I'm positive you like it when I do this," he said as he settled deeply inside her.

Her eyes met his. She could feel them glazing over, but there was still one more thing she needed to tell him.

"I'm in dairy," she said before he started to move and she lost the ability to speak at all.

7

THE SOUND OF RAIN DRUMMED at Chance.

On some level, he knew he was dreaming, but it didn't matter. He wanted to stay exactly where he was. Deep inside Tiffany, his hands gliding over the smooth silkiness of her hips as she moved with him.

He struggled against consciousness, but the rain wouldn't stop and he found it increasingly hard to ignore.

He dragged open his eyes and brightened considerably when he realized he was in Tiffany's bed. Why mourn the loss of the dream, he thought, when he could have the real thing?

He turned, intending to reach for Tiffany, but her side of the bed was empty aside from a tangle of white cotton sheets.

The rain stopped abruptly and he realized the incessant sound of falling water hadn't been rain at all but the shower.

Too bad he hadn't awakened earlier or he could have joined Tiffany under the spray. Thinking about her beautiful body slick with water was enough to make him hard.

He smiled at his body's reaction. He'd always thought he had more self-control than the average male, but he could well be on his way to setting a record for number of erections in a twenty-four hour period.

It was certainly a personal record.

He propped himself up on the pillows and put his hands behind his head, content to wait for Tiffany to emerge from the bathroom, which adjoined the small bedroom.

Maybe he could talk her into slipping out of her towel and coming back to bed. He was more than ready to change his view that staying in bed too late, even on a Saturday morning, was a poor use of time.

The door swung open a moment later, and he craned his head, eager for that first glimpse of her in a state of undress.

But instead of a towel, she was wearing a way-too-modest short-sleeved shirt and blue-jean shorts at least four or five inches longer than he'd have liked them.

She'd applied a subtle shade of lipstick and, he guessed, light makeup. Her hair, which fell past her shoulders in straight, wet strands, was the only part of her that wasn't ready for, say, a trip to the mall.

"You're dressed," he said in a deflated voice.

Her head whipped around. "You're awake," she said.

Her cheeks were flushed almost as though she were...embarrassed?

He frowned. After the things they'd done to each other last night, that didn't make sense. But neither did her getting dressed in a steamy bathroom instead of in front of him.

"I didn't get much sleep last night," he said and could have sworn the dull red of her cheeks deepened.

He saw her swallow. "Neither did I."

He arched an eyebrow and made his voice go soft. "That's why I think you should come back to bed."

The invitation hung between them, heavy with a meaning Chance thought was perfectly clear. Her eyes touched on his and in them he saw the desire that could flare so easily between them, but then she looked away.

"I thought we'd go to the St. Patrick's Day parade." She moved swiftly to her dresser and picked up what looked to be a pair of pierced earrings. "It's this morning."

I thought we'd make love all morning. Chance nearly spoke the thought aloud but her demeanor stopped him.

She reminded him of a skittish cat ready to shy away, maybe for good, if he pressed too hard. He couldn't figure it out. Not after last night. But there it was.

"I love a parade," he said truthfully, although he hadn't been to one since...he didn't remember when. His only memories were of the grand productions televised each Thanksgiving Day.

Could his parents have been so adamant that he and his brother chase success that they'd begun conditioning them in childhood to avoid the frivolous?

Doing his best to mask his disappointment that Tiffany wasn't rejoining him in bed, Chance swung his legs off the mattress. Maybe the parade would be fun.

"Just give me a couple minutes to get ready," he said.

She averted her eyes when he reached for the shorts at the foot of the bed and pulled them on. He couldn't shake the impression that she was making a show of concentration as she put on her earrings.

"I need to go downstairs and get my things," he added, partly to see if she'd look at him.

She didn't. "Uh-huh," she said.

"To hell with this," he muttered under his breath and was across the room in three strides.

The eyes that flew to his were startled. Her mouth parted, her breath quickened and the pulse jumped beneath the fine skin of her throat.

He'd intended to haul her into his arms but found that he couldn't. Not if that's not where she wanted to be.

"Did you want something?" she asked after a breathless moment.

Yeah, he wanted a lot of things. Not the least of which was not to be treated like a stranger after the intimate things they'd done. But maybe that was unrealistic because strangers, after all, were what they were.

He didn't even know what she did for a living.

"What did you mean last night, when you said you were in dairy?" he asked.

She swallowed and again he saw the pulse jump in

her neck. "I work for the Iowa Dairy League," she said.

"Iowa," he stated. That made sense. She had a wholesome quality about her that fit with his image of the state. "Where in Iowa?"

"I was born in the northeast part of the state, outside Waterloo," she said, which brought up a host of other questions. Did she live there now? What exactly did she do for the dairy league? Had she always liked cattle?

"How about you?"

"Atlanta," he answered and quickly realized he couldn't afford to reveal anything more about himself.

He couldn't very well tell her he was an attorney in Washington, D.C., the Starched Suit capital of the world. Not when that described the type of man she most wanted to avoid.

"Where's your Southern accent then?" she asked.

"I keep it in a jar beside my bed," he said, putting on a thick one, "and only take it out when I'm trying to get a pretty woman to give me a good-morning kiss."

He reached out to run a fingertip down her cheek and over her mouth, realizing he was trying to distract her from asking any more questions. Instead he managed to distract himself.

"Is that right?" she asked in a voice that trembled.

He wanted that kiss, and much more, quite desperately, had wanted it since he'd awakened from dreaming of her.

"Believe me when I tell you I ain't just whistling Dixie," he said, giving her a grin not much steadier than her voice.

She laughed, an unexpected sound that went straight to his heart. The distance that had sprung up between them disappeared and she looped her arms around his neck, leaned forward and kissed him with the familiarity of a lover.

His body reacted the same way it did every time they touched: with enthusiasm. The heat flowed, the excitement built, the sensations overwhelmed.

He fisted his hands in her damp hair, breathed in her strawberry-scented shampoo and explored her mouth. What was happening to him? Why couldn't he get enough of this? Of her?

After long moments, she drew back. They smiled at each other and, just like that, the awkwardness of the morning was gone.

"Considering the half-naked man in your bedroom, you sure you want to go to that parade?" he asked, wiggling his eyebrows suggestively.

She ran her hand down his chest and over his flat stomach, but stopped shy of the waistband of his shorts. "The parade only happens once a year," she said huskily. "I'm sure I can persuade the man to get naked more often than that."

He laughed and drew back.

"I'll hold you to it," he said before he turned. Despite still being aroused, he went downstairs whistling.

And the tune wasn't Dixie.

TIFFANY SWITCHED OFF the blow-dryer, wishing she could turn off her mind as easily.

She rolled her eyes at her reflection in the mirror.

She was fresh from a night of great sex with a hot guy. Why couldn't she leave it at that? Why did she have to overanalyze every little thing?

Like the way he'd asked her to expand on her revelation that she was in dairy. If he hadn't wanted to know anything about her, would he have asked what she meant?

Maybe he'd intended the question to take the mystery out of their relationship by opening up a give-and-take. Maybe he'd wanted her to ask him more about his upbringing in Atlanta than why she couldn't detect a Southern accent.

She'd quite possibly bypassed a golden opportunity to find out about the man she was sleeping with. He'd probably have answered any of her questions, no matter how silly.

She put her hands on her hips, cocked her head and once again addressed her mirror image.

"If you were a tree, what kind of tree would you be?"

She giggled at herself. No way would she ask that question. At least not first. She'd start with the nuts and bolts, like where he lived and what he'd done at his last job.

Before she could lose her nerve, she headed for the stairs, thinking about how to start the questioning. If she hooked her arms around his neck, she could set a friendly tone. She frowned because the tone might be too friendly.

If they started kissing, she might not get the first question out.

No. It would be better to march up to him and be up front about what she wanted to know.

"Sure, I can meet you this afternoon." Chance's voice drifted up the stairs, stopping her before she'd descended more than a single step. "Name a time and I'll be there."

Disappointment washed over her like the spray from this morning's shower. Who was he talking to? And why was he offering to meet someone when they had plans to go to the parade?

"That sounds fine," he said and paused. "Yes, I know the place. I'll meet you there."

Who would he meet where? she wanted to know and barely stopped herself from running down the stairs and demanding he tell her. Instead she waited, barely moving, hoping to get another clue.

The silence stretched from seconds to what must have been a full minute until she concluded that he'd hung up the phone. Bracing herself, she continued down the stairs, slowing when she caught sight of him sitting on the sofa.

He was naked aside from the shorts he'd pulled on a few minutes before, his body so toned she could see the ridges in his stomach muscles and hard definition of his biceps. Her knees would have gone weak at the magnificent sight of him if he didn't have a cell phone in his hand.

He looked up, spotted her and raised a finger to indicate he'd be with her in a minute. He didn't say anything, not even when he switched off the phone, clueing her that he'd been checking his messages.

His frown was so deep, she could have drowned in it.

"Is something wrong?" she asked.

Drat. Of all the questions she'd meant to ask, that hadn't been one of them.

"Not really." He dropped the phone back into his worn leather bag. "Just a couple messages from my father. He's concerned because he hasn't heard from me."

"Does your father—"

"—annoy the hell out of me? Yes, he does," he finished for her, but that wasn't what she'd been about to ask. She'd wanted to know if his father knew where he was.

But Chance quite clearly didn't want to talk about his father. At least, not to her.

Lord, she was a fool. Of course he didn't want to share the details of his life. She should have figured that much when he hadn't deigned to explain the most minor of details, like his lack of a Southern accent.

They'd had sex. A meeting of the bodies that didn't obligate either party to disclose anything about their minds. Other people had sex all the time without the need to play twenty questions. Why couldn't she?

"Tiffany, there's something I have to tell you."

She started, so lost in her thoughts that she was surprised to find he was standing directly in front of her. The blinds were still drawn, keeping out the sunlight, and in the semidarkness his variable eyes looked neither blue nor green but gray.

"You can't come to the parade today," she said.

He grimaced. "How did you know that?"

"I heard you making plans to meet somebody when I was coming down the stairs."

Something shifted behind his eyes and she guessed he was wondering if that had been all she'd heard. She waited a moment, but he didn't offer an explanation.

"It's okay," she said as though she was cool with being kept in the dark. "I'll go to the parade without you, maybe hang out with Susie if she's not too busy."

He put his hands on her shoulders, and she was amazed that even that brief contact had her wanting to drag him off to bed. Or, failing that, over to the bottom of the stairs. Despite the fact that he was virtually a stranger.

"You sure you're okay with it?"

"Perfectly," she said with false cheerfulness, exactly like a woman in the midst of a no-strings affair should. She knew she didn't imagine the relief that passed over his face.

"How about if we hook up later tonight?"

"Sure."

Her smile felt so brittle it was a wonder her teeth didn't crack, but he didn't seem to notice. He kissed her swiftly on the lips, and then took the stairs two by two, probably thinking about making a quick getaway.

Don't go, her inner voice cried. *Spend the day with me.*
"Chance."

What was the matter with her? Tiffany thought as Chance stopped and turned, giving her a great view of his long, muscular legs and broad, beautiful chest. Surely she couldn't mean to speak her mind?

"Yeah?" he asked.

She hesitated, unsure of what she was going to say until the words were out.

"I think you should call your father," she said. "Tell him you're okay."

He considered her for a moment and she had the fleeting feeling that he was about to share a confidence, but then he nodded once and disappeared up the stairs.

She gazed up at the empty space where he'd been, telling herself that what had just happened was okay with her.

She was getting exactly what she'd sought: A no-strings fling with a good-time guy.

The right to demand answers from him wasn't part of the deal.

AT SHORTLY BEFORE ONE that afternoon, Chance stood at the entrance of a hotel lounge that featured gleaming mahogany and polished wood floors and scanned the growing crowd.

The airline had recovered his luggage and he was dressed in a light-gray, tropical-weight wool suit with cuffed trousers and a single-breasted jacket tailored so it didn't pinch his shoulders. His shirt was a darker gray, his tie silk, his shoes Italian leather.

Tiffany would probably run screaming in the opposite direction if she got a look at him.

He thrust aside the thought and again focused on the Dixieland Lounge, which was inside the elegant historic district hotel where he'd secured a room by slipping the desk clerk a substantial cash incentive.

He'd worry about Tiffany after he made amends with Mary Greeley, the congressman's daughter who was, after all, the reason he was in town.

If only he could find her.

The bar was filling up, probably because the parade was over or nearly so, and there was enough green to blind a grasshopper. Lime-colored streamers hung from the drink racks above the bar, and the tam-o'-shanter-wearing bartender had dyed his mustache and goatee green.

"Looking for me, sugar?"

He turned and saw cleavage. Bared by a skintight green dress at least a size too small, the cleavage demanded to be seen and admired. As did the woman, who appeared to be in her late twenties. She had long, blond hair no doubt helped along by a bottle, an hourglass figure and a face pretty enough to get her anything she wanted.

"I'm looking for a client," he said.

"If you're Chauncy McMann, that'd be me," she said, sticking out a manicured hand. "Mary Greeley."

She was congressman Jake Greeley's daughter?

Chance masked his surprise and took her hand, pretending not to notice the way she hung on to his too long. She seemed the antithesis of a congressman's daughter, but maybe that was the point. Maybe it was exactly the image she was trying to cultivate.

"Nice to meet you," he said, careful to keep his manner professional as he shoved the hand she'd been grasping in his jacket pocket. "I'm only sorry it wasn't yesterday."

"Me, too," she said, wetting lips that were painted cherry red. "What happened?"

He'd spent the day exploring the beach and Tiffany and hadn't remembered to reschedule his appointment with Mary until he'd checked the messages on his cell phone that morning. Not only had congressman Greeley called to find out what was going on, so had his father. Three times.

He still couldn't believe he'd forgotten. Even after he decided to indulge himself yesterday, he hadn't intended to take the day off from the responsibilities of being a lawyer. He'd still meant to figure out how best to proceed with Mary's case.

"It's been crazy," he said, sticking to the truth. "The airline lost my luggage and I had trouble with my hotel and rental-car reservations."

"Ah, I'm getting the picture," she said, laying a hand on his arm as they walked to a table. "St. Patrick's Festival syndrome."

"That's as good a name for it as any," he said as he helped her onto a tall stool and took the one across

An Important Message from the Editors

Dear Reader,

Because you've chosen to read one of our fine romance novels, we'd like to say "thank you!" And, as a special way to thank you, we're offering you a choice between the books you love so well OR those from a similar series that other readers like yourself just can't get enough of... Indicate your preference and we'll send you your choice of Two Free Books plus an exciting Mystery Gift, absolutely FREE!

Please enjoy them with our compliments...

Pam Powers

P.S. And because we value our customers, we've attached something extra inside...

Peel off Seal and Place Inside...

EDITOR'S FREE GIFT SEAL THANK YOU

HARLEQUIN®
Live the emotion™

...ween...

...r Harlequin® Blaze™

...k from one of our fine romance
...ft: a choice of **2 FREE Books**
...ying OR **2 FREE Books** from
...e yourself also love.

...Gift Seal from the front cover
...at right.
...r your 2 FREE Books.
...automatically send you
...tery Gift!

...Harlequin Temptation®
...FREE BOOKS from this sassy,
...eductive series!

...e™
...n the
...ads!

...ect, your **2 FREE BOOKS**
...rice of **$8.50 or more**
...r more in Canada.

...OKMARK. And remember…
...e Gift Offer, we'll send you
...OLUTELY FREE!

With Our Compliments
The Editors

from her. "Now why don't you tell me about this lady who's suing you."

She tossed back her long, blond hair and gave him a disbelieving smile.

"Not until I have a drink." She lifted a hand to signal a waiter. "I'm not much for parades, but I love to party. And this is the day for it."

A half hour later, after Mary was well into her second vodka martini, Chance finally had her version of the story.

She'd rear-ended another motorist at a red light. Because the woman appeared uninjured and the damage to her car minimal, Georgia state law didn't require an accident report. Mary hadn't wanted the hassle of dealing with the insurance company so she'd written the other woman a check at the scene to cover the damages to her car. It had come as a shock when the woman later claimed whiplash and threatened to file suit.

"I'll set up a meeting with," he paused to check his notes, "Betsy Leland. This should be a simple matter to resolve. Your father's private investigator got photos of her doing tai chi on her back porch. Once she sees those, she should agree to settle out of court."

Mary took another pull of her drink. "Why settle at all if you can prove she doesn't have whiplash?"

"Your father wants this thing to go away," Chance said.

She leaned against the high back of the tall chair and crossed her legs, almost as though she were posing.

"Tell me something, Chauncy McMann," she said as she swirled the skinny straw in her drink. The lashes framing the blue eyes she rose to his were expertly made up. "Why did my father send you?"

"It's a legal matter and I'm an attorney."

"No." She shook her head so that the blonde strands swung. "Why did he send *you* and not some other attorney?"

"I'm based in D.C. but I also have a license to practice law in Georgia," he said.

"Oh, come now." She put down her glass and leaned over the table, providing him with an eye-popping view of cleavage. "Daddy doesn't operate like that. There must be some other connection."

"He and my father went to law school together, if that's what you mean," Chance stated.

She gave a soft laugh. "That sounds more like Daddy. I take it he's counting on you to keep this quiet so it doesn't come out that I was drinking and driving and somehow damage his sterling reputation by association."

Chance tried to hide his surprise that she'd been drinking. Why hadn't Jake Greeley told him that beforehand? "I don't abuse attorney-client privilege."

"For the record, I wasn't drinking. Not then, anyway. That's just another of the false claims Betsy Leland is making against me."

"Why would she do that?"

"My guess is money," Mary said. "I shouldn't have given her such a generous amount. She obviously made the connection that Daddy's a politician with deep pockets and figured she could get more."

"Probably. But she doesn't have much of a case. The only evidence she has is the check you wrote her." Chance slipped his papers back into his briefcase. "That's all the information I need. Thanks for meeting with me."

"You're not planning to leave, are you?" Mary reached across the table and lightly stroked his hand. "Not when the business is over and the pleasure's about to begin. Something tells me you and I could have a good time together."

Her eyes met his in a bold look and he had little doubt of her meaning. She wanted sex. The no-questions-asked, no-commitment kind of sex. The kind he'd half convinced himself he and Tiffany had had that morning.

But there was an ocean of difference between Mary and Tiffany, an ocean he didn't want to cross.

"Don't tell me you're going to give me the song-and-dance about making sure we keep things professional between us," Mary said, walking her fingers up his arm. "Daddy won't find out. I can be discreet, too."

He clenched his jaw and not because he was suffering from the effects of sexual attraction.

"I'm flattered," he said, "but I already have plans for tonight."

She laughed and withdrew her hand.

"What am I? Too wild for you?" she asked, bringing the drink to her lips and taking a lusty swallow.

8

TIFFANY TRIED NOT TO CROWD the far wall in a booth for two at the downtown Savannah nightspot where she was supposed to meet Chance. So Savannah and the people invading it had gone crazy. It was nothing she couldn't handle.

"I'll have to say no to that," she told the skinny, middle-aged man regarding her with a hopeful expression from beside the booth.

"Aw, shucks." His lean face fell into a comically miserable expression. "You're the fifth woman who said no. Tell me something. What am I doing wrong?"

"Let's see," Tiffany said as though she actually had to think about it. She snapped her fingers. "I've got it. You're asking women you don't know if they'd take off their clothes so you can paint them green."

He removed his green plastic hat and scratched a head that appeared to be losing hair fast. Then he took a quick scan of the noisy, packed bar and his expression cleared.

"Hey, thanks for the advice, but I gotta go." He jammed the hat back on his head. "I see a woman over there I know."

She congratulated herself on handling the situation

as he walked away, his swagger back. His request hadn't even been the wildest one she'd fielded that day.

That distinction went to the man who'd tossed her a pair of green pasties and told her he hoped to see her during amateur night at the Bare Bottom Lounge. The fan favorite would be invited to strip there regularly, he promised.

As the day wore on, Tiffany tried very hard to convince herself she wouldn't have liked the sleepy, Southern, boring Savannah better.

Even though the greening of the city rendered things like pancakes and grits inedible, it was a cute theme. And the parade had been fun, with the bagpipers, marching bands and long line of sometimes garishly decorated floats.

She could have done without some of the craziness, notably way too many people drinking way too much alcohol.

But she'd handled it. She'd even ordered the kellygreen ginger ale instead of opting for the regular variety.

Yep, she was handling everything just fine, including Chance and their casual, steaming-hot affair. She might not be a prototypical wild woman, but she was wild enough. Why else would she have stripped for Chance and made wild love with him on the staircase?

Why else would she have oh-so-urbanely restrained from asking him who he was meeting this afternoon instead of jealously demanding assurance it wasn't a woman?

Oh, please God, don't let it have been a woman.

"There you are." A familiar voice snapped her out of her reverie and Tiffany gazed up to see Susie standing beside the booth. "Thank heaven you left word where you'd be this time."

Tiffany made a point of looking over her friend's shoulder. "Somebody chasing you?"

"I sure hope not," Susie said, scooting into the booth opposite her. She had to shout to be heard. "But Kyle'll have my head if he knows I'm here. He says I should stay out of your business."

Hallelujah.

Tiffany wasn't sure whether to be glad that the music filling the place suddenly stopped. Probably not. That didn't mean she had to let Susie choose the topic of conversation.

"Has the tourism bureau ever considered approaching the dairy companies about a tie-in to the festival?" Tiffany asked, airing an idea that had been dancing around in her head. "I'm thinking green milk cartons instead of green milk because of the looks-like-it-could-be-curdled factor."

"Hey, that's not a bad idea," Susie put her elbows on the table and leaned forward. "But not why I came to see you."

"I was afraid of that," Tiffany muttered.

"You know how much I care about you, right?" Susie didn't wait for an answer but plunged ahead. "I don't want to see you hurt."

Tiffany gave up trying to avoid the subject and

made her voice sound skeptical. "And you think Chance can hurt me?"

"I think an *affair* could hurt you," Susie said. "I know you, Tiffany. You take things seriously. I'm not saying that's bad. It's one of the things I love about you. But other people aren't like you. Things don't mean as much to them."

"Gosh, Susie, you make me sound naive. I've grown up since high school. I know what Chance and I have is purely sexual."

Tiffany tried not to cringe at the way she sounded and mentally congratulated herself for joining the ranks of modern women instead.

"You do?" Susie sounded skeptical. "You know it's just sex, and that's okay with you?"

"Of course it is." Tiffany reached across the table and covered her friend's hand before Susie could lodge another protest. "You know what else is okay with me? That one of my oldest and dearest friends is a busybody. That way, I know how much she loves me."

Susie's lips curled into a wry smile. "You sure know how to flatter a girl."

Tiffany laughed. "Chance will be here any minute. I'd invite you to stay but something tells me you don't want Kyle to find you here."

"You're right about that." Susie did a mock eye roll. "Would you believe he thinks I'm a busybody, too?"

"No," Tiffany said, bringing both hands to her cheeks as though it couldn't be possible. The two friends smiled at each other.

Susie scooted over on the bench seat but paused before she reached the end. "I almost forgot. A couple of girls we went to high school with live in Savannah. I mentioned you were in town when I ran into them yesterday and they want to meet for drinks tomorrow night. What do you think?"

"Don't you have festival stuff to do?"

"Some," Susie said, "But tomorrow's Sunday so the weekend will be almost over. I can spare some time for happy hour."

Tiffany hesitated.

"You can bring Chance along if you like," Susie said.

"Was I that obvious?" Tiffany gave a self-deprecating laugh. "Of course I'll come. And I'll bring Chance. If he's not busy, that is."

"Great," Susie said as she got out of the booth. "Now I better get out of here before Kyle figures out where I am and says this proves I'm a meddler."

"That's probably wise," Tiffany said.

Susie sprang out of the booth like she was springloaded, leaned over to give Tiffany a quick hug and then shot her a worried look.

"I hope you know what you're doing," she said and then she was gone, leaving Tiffany to mull over what she'd said.

Most of it, unfortunately, was true. Tiffany didn't normally take anything, let alone love and sex, lightly. That's probably why, until Chance, she could have counted the times she'd had sex on the fingers of one hand.

The encounters hadn't been unpleasant, but she hadn't been eager to repeat the experiences.

She put her chin in her hands. Maybe she was fooling herself about this thing she had going with Chance. Maybe she couldn't continue it.

"Now don't you look prettier than a prize-winning rose?"

The male voice, heavy with the sounds of the South, came from beside the booth. Preparing herself to good-naturedly send yet another pushy man on his way, she sighed and lifted her head.

The rejection caught in her throat when she saw that the man was Chance. He was holding a mug of frothing green beer and grinning, maybe because he'd fooled her with that exaggerated accent.

His eyes were smiling, as though they, and not the sun, had the power to warm her. In blue jeans and a black shirt that accentuated the breadth of his chest, he looked solid and strong and so very handsome.

If he asked to paint her naked body green, she'd say yes. As long as he did it in private with washable paints and quick access to a shower.

"Hi," she said.

"Hi, yourself." He set his mug down on the table before he slid into the booth. Not across from her as Susie had done but right next to her so that the entire delectable length of him was touching her.

Her nerve endings danced, her blood bubbled, heat pooled low inside her and she kissed him.

Just reached up, tangled her fingers in his hair to hold his head steady and kissed him as though it had been a year instead of only hours since she'd seen him. Their mouths opened, their tongues tangled and the bar disappeared.

Until a microphone squeaked, reminding her that they were in a bar where a live band was scheduled to perform at any minute. Shocked by her lack of control, she drew back and mentally amended her thoughts of a moment ago.

Maybe Susie was wrong and she could, too, enjoy a purely sexual affair.

"Now that's the way a man likes to be greeted," Chance said, his features softening with a passion he didn't bother to hide. He gathered her close with an arm around her shoulders and it felt as though she was exactly where she belonged.

When the band broke into a rock-and-roll version of "Waltzing Matilda," she felt his body vibrate with laughter. "They must not realize that song's Australian."

He'd spoken near her ear and his warm breath was so intoxicating it was all she could do to smile and nod. If the band hadn't been loud enough to prevent conversation, she probably would have babbled.

Chance picked up his mug of green beer and took a healthy swallow. She watched his throat muscles work, thinking even they were sexy. She took a gulp of ginger ale.

The band's lead singer bounded into the aisles of the bar with a cordless microphone. As he went, he shoved the mike in front of whoever happened to be in his path so an audience member could sing a few lines.

When the singer was a few paces from their booth, he stopped and held the microphone out like an offering.

Chance put down his beer, winked at her, slid out of the booth and grabbed the mike before anyone else could.

He knew the words, she had to hand him that much. He was even roughly on key, his voice so low and sexy it wouldn't have mattered even if he wasn't.

He sang a few lines, moving as sensually to the music as he had when he'd been playing the sax. She was so caught up in the pleasure of watching him that she didn't realize he was moving toward her until he held the microphone out to her.

As though he expected her to sing.

Her. Tiffany Albright. Dairy lobbyist and congressman's daughter.

She swallowed. She couldn't. She wouldn't.

When she shook her head, he immediately backed off. A moment later, he handed the microphone to an eager young girl in shorts and a neon-green halter top.

"Watching old Hilda, Watching old Hilda," the girl belted out. She obviously knew as little about Australian folk songs as the band knew about the Irish.

Or as Tiffany knew about having an affair with a wild man.

"Let's get out of here," Chance said instead of rejoining her in the booth, slowly enough that she could read his lips. He put out a hand and she took it, holding tightly to him as he wove through the crowd and out into the night.

The bar had been warm but the night was so balmy it was barely an improvement.

Or maybe she was too warm because she always felt that way with Chance. Her sizzling attraction to him was why she'd kissed him in the bar and why it made perfect sense for her to have sex with him.

Their relationship, after all, was all about sex.

She sent him a sidelong glance, noticing how the moonlight gave him a sensual glow. The sooner they had sex, she thought with a sensual shiver, the better.

The street was crowded and noisy, but not nearly as noisy as the bar had been. She was a modern woman. A woman who let her needs be known. She'd tell him now. Before she completely lost her nerve.

"Chance," she said, tugging on his hand. She took a deep breath for courage and plunged ahead. "Let's have sex."

"Maybe later," Chance said.

OF ALL THE THINGS TIFFANY thought Chance might say to her proposition, that hadn't been one of them.

Maybe later?

Admittedly she didn't have a lot of experience in these things, but that didn't sound like something a lover should say. She'd expected him to respond with an answer that was at least mildly positive.

And, she thought crossly, to look at her instead of over her shoulder. She got the impression he was checking out another woman he'd want to have sex with now. Heck, maybe he'd spotted the woman he'd met with that afternoon.

"You're a real jerk," she said, biting her lip to stop it from trembling. That, at least, seemed to get through to him. His eyes swung to hers, filled with what was obviously confusion.

"I am?" he asked, but clearly her opinion was of little importance because whatever he'd been looking at before claimed his attention once again.

"Yeah," she bit out unhappily, "you are."

"Can we talk about this later?" he asked absently, placing a hand on her shoulder. For a fleeting moment, she thought he meant to console her, but the gentle pressure he exerted made it clear he was trying to steer her aside.

She stubbornly dug in her heels, but he went around her. She spun, intending to give him another piece of her mind, but saw what he'd been looking at instead.

Two large men who could have been the stars of WrestleMania stood facing each other, as alike as twins except one had a shaved head while the other sported untidy, brown hair as long as hers. They each held the arm of a petite woman with short, spiky black hair. She was dressed in a halter top and shorts that barely covered her rear end.

"Let me go," the woman cried, trying to pull away.

One of the WrestleMania twins yanked her arm so roughly that Tiffany winced. "You ain't goin' nowhere unless it's with me," he yelled.

"That's what you think," the other man bellowed. "She's leaving with me."

Tiffany had a clear view of the ugly scene because the people crowding the sidewalks veered away from the trio. The notable exception was Chance, who was rushing toward them.

Her pulse gave a wild leap. Couldn't he see that each of the men had three or four inches and thirty or forty pounds on him? Couldn't he tell their testosterone was raging and their brains had gone on vacation?

"Chance, wait!" she called but his ground-eating steps didn't even slow.

She hurried forward but Chance had enough of a head start that she had little hope of reaching him before he got to the trio.

"You heard the lady," Chance said in a voice that rang with authority. "Let her go."

Tiffany wanted to yell at Chance to back down but the words stuck in her throat.

The hulking look-alikes continued to tug at the woman like very large, very angry dogs fighting over a bone.

"Let her go," Chance repeated, even more forcefully, "or I'll make you let her go."

Was he crazy? He should have hunted down a cop and alerted him to what was happening. Enough of them were patrolling River Street, although Tiffany had to admit she hadn't seen one in the last few minutes.

Neither man released the pixie, but the big, bald

one turned toward Chance. "You'll make me, huh?" he asked, his disbelieving voice slurred with drink.

Tiffany had the impression of narrowed eyes, a lip with a mean curl and a dull, splotchy complexion before a motion to the man's right caught her attention. It was his counterpart's fist, sailing over the petite woman's head and slamming into the side of his face.

The stricken man howled in outrage at the same time he let go of the woman's arm. He cocked his own fist while he yelled invectives. The long-haired man shoved the woman aside and positioned his hands in front of him like a boxer.

The woman staggered but didn't fall, prompting Tiffany to rush to her side. "Are you okay?" she asked.

"Why wouldn't I be?" the woman answered roughly, the alcohol on her breath nearly knocking Tiffany over.

"Hey, break it up," Chance yelled, bringing Tiffany's attention back to the dueling men. They were circling each other with their fists raised.

The big, bald bully reared back with a punch that sent the long-haired thug straight at Chance. The long-haired man, who also seemed to be drunk, swung wildly as he tried to right himself.

"Chance, look out," Tiffany yelled.

Chance turned his shoulders and moved his head to one side, but not before the long-haired man's fist connected with his jaw with enough power to fell a tree. He swayed but the blow must have been glancing because he kept his feet and raised his own fists.

"What in the hell does he think he's doing?" the woman muttered as she plowed her fingers through her short, spiky hair. Up close, she appeared to be no more than eighteen or nineteen years old. The hulks fighting over her couldn't have been much older.

"Somebody's gonna get hurt," Chance warned, but he could have been talking to the Savannah moon for all the attention the men paid him.

Like a bull with a matador in his sights, the bald one rushed his long-haired foe. He reared back, preparing to let another punch fly. The long-haired man stepped aside at the last instant but was so drunk he fell to the pavement.

The bald man had already let his punch sail. Chance tried to lean away, but he wasn't quick enough. The bald man's fist collided with his face with a sickening thud.

Chance reeled, clutching his right eye. The long-haired man lay moaning on the pavement, showing no inclination to continue the fight.

"Ah, hell," the bald man yelled at Chance. "Now why did you have to go and get in the way for?"

"Yeah," the woman said, rushing at Chance. Tiffany trailed after her, wondering what was going on.

"What did you think you were doing, you jerk?" the black-haired woman demanded of Chance.

"Helping you," Chance answered.

"Helping me?" The woman had a little-girl voice so high-pitched and angry Tiffany wouldn't have been surprised had she stomped her foot. "I didn't need your help."

"Sure looked like it to me," Chance said.

"Those men were getting ready to fight over you," Tiffany interjected, positioning herself between Chance and the angry pixie.

"Me and Pete like to fight," the bald man said with an unhappy cast to his mouth. The long-haired man, who must've been Pete, groaned what sounded like agreement from his prone position on the sidewalk.

"And I like to watch them fight," the woman said, still fuming.

"You know these guys?" Tiffany asked the young woman.

"Sure do." The woman hugged the bald man's arm. "Brad here's my boyfriend." She indicated the fallen man with a nod of her head. "And Pete there's my other boyfriend."

"Help me up, Brad?" Pete asked from the sidewalk.

Brad reached down, gripped Pete's hand in a secure, beefy grasp and hoisted him to his feet. The woman was immediately beside him, examining the place on his arm he'd skinned raw when he fell.

"Next time, mind your own business," she snapped at Chance.

"Well, if that don't beat all," Chance said as the drunken trio tottered away. The pixie and Brad flanked Pete, who had his arms around them for support. "I guess I miscalculated there."

"Guess so." Tiffany brushed his hair back from his forehead while she anxiously inspected his damaged eye. The tissue around it had already started to swell and bruise. "You're going to have a black eye."

"I figured that." He sounded nonchalant, as though he got socked in the eye every other day. Maybe he did, but the way he'd marched into the fray against two bigger men was still one of the bravest, most fool-hardy things she'd ever seen.

"Tell me something," she said, searching his face. "What possessed you to do that?"

"Somebody had to." He gave her a sheepish look. "At least, I thought somebody had to."

But he was the only one who had. That fact slammed into her with the power of the punch Brad had thrown at Chance.

All afternoon, she'd tried to convince herself that all she felt for Chance was physical attraction.

It probably hadn't been true before but it was even less true now. Yes, he was a wild man. Wild enough that he'd been ready to fight bigger men without re-gard to his own safety because he thought a woman was in danger.

Even though she saw the folly in that, she couldn't help but admire it. She couldn't help but admire *him.* Never mind that the cause hadn't been as just as he'd believed.

He smiled at her despite his banged-up face. "Sorry I walked away from you earlier. What was it you wanted to say?"

"It was nothing," she said, waving her hand dis-missively.

"You sure?" he asked, then scrunched up his brow. "I thought you called me a jerk."

"Oh, no." She shook her head. "You must not have

heard right. I said...those men over there are going berserk."

He looked even more puzzled. "But how could you have seen them? The way you were standing, your back was to—"

"That woman was the one who called you a jerk," she blurted out to deflect his attention from herself.

He winced. "Yeah, right. She did."

Tiffany immediately felt ashamed of herself for pointing out exactly how ungrateful the woman had been. She took his hand and squeezed it.

"Don't worry about her." Tiffany nodded in the direction in which the woman had headed with the hulking look-alikes. In the distance, the drunken trio was singing about bottles of green beer on the wall. "She wouldn't know a good man if he rushed to her rescue."

Chance's eyes searched hers, the moonlight illuminating his damaged face. In addition to the blackening eye, he had a cut on his jaw that trickled blood. But when he smiled, she thought she'd never seen a more handsome man.

"What do you say we get you back to my place so we can put some ice on that eye?" she asked through a throat that suddenly felt thick.

"I wouldn't say no," he said softly.

Neither would she say no to him. Not for as long as they were both in Savannah. For once in her life, she was going to use both hands and grab what life threw at her and not worry about the consequences.

Even though she knew she'd eventually have to throw it back.

9

CHANCE TRIED NOT TO WINCE when Tiffany dabbed the cut on his jaw with an antiseptic-soaked cotton ball, but he couldn't help it. The stuff stung.

"Hold still," she ordered as she continued to dab but couldn't hide the ghost of a smile. "I swear you men are all alike. Bash you in the face and you're fine. But put antiseptic on your cut and it's like you're being tortured with acid."

"It feels like acid," he said, gritting his teeth. "And why was a guy like Brad wearing a ring anyway? Who did he think he was? Mr. T?"

"Mr. Who?"

"Mr. T," Chance repeated. "That guy on the commercials who wears enough jewelry to bust a metal detector. Used to be on the A-Team."

"The what kind of team?"

"You don't watch much TV, do you?" Neither did he but stations that aired televised sports seemed to like the big guy's commercials. "Mr. T's like Mike Tyson without the boxing gloves. Or the lisp. Or the ring, come to think of it. Seems to me he used to wrestle."

"Then if that'd been Mr. T on the street, you'd be in the hospital instead of sitting in my kitchen with ice on your eye."

"Thanks for the vote of confidence," he muttered.

She stroked the uninjured side of his face with a soft, sure touch. "You don't need my vote," she said, looking straight into his good eye. "I already elected you."

She sent him a sweet smile before reaching into the box of bandages on the table, pulling one out and leaning across him to cover the cut on his jaw.

"Ow," he said.

"Baby."

"I told you. It hurts."

"It hurts me, too," she said, stroking his good cheek before she started methodically gathering the first-aid supplies.

She was really something, Chance thought as he watched her work. Sweet and sexy. Tough and loyal. And unpredictable. Oh, yeah, he couldn't forget unpredictable.

He doubted any of the other women he knew had the guts to take a chance on a stranger, the way Tiffany had gambled with him. Except perhaps Mary Greeley, but he'd realized earlier today that Tiffany wasn't at all like Mary.

Tiffany had nerve, yes, but she also had a surprising dose of naiveté, which was one of the things he liked best about her.

She'd said she wanted to have a fling with a good-time guy, but after being around her for a few days the claim didn't ring true. She seemed like a woman who'd match up perfectly with a suit-and-tie guy. Like him.

"Let me ask you something," she said and he got ready to give an honest answer. It was past time he did. "Back there on the street, why didn't you try to find a cop?"

He frowned, disappointed that she hadn't asked a personal question until he realized that she was trying to figure out how his mind worked. Too bad he'd have to tell her it didn't work very well.

"I didn't think of it," he said. "I saw a woman I thought was in trouble and I reacted."

"I always think before I react," she said softly.

He laughed. "Oh, come on. How about the first time you saw me? When I was playing the sax? That kiss seemed awfully impulsive."

She shook her head.

"It wasn't. Not really. I wouldn't have approached you if I hadn't decided I was sick of all the boring men in Washington, D.C."

Chance's entire body tensed. "Washington, D.C.?" he said, trying to sound casual. "Why'd you mention D.C.? Don't you live in Iowa?"

She leaned back in the kitchen chair and regarded him. "I was born in Iowa. I live in D.C."

"You said you worked for the Iowa Dairy League."

"I do," she said. "As a lobbyist."

"On Capitol Hill?"

"That's a typical hangout for D.C. lobbyists," she said with a wry smile.

He knew that. Just as he knew that Tiffany residing in the district should have been good news. He already wanted to continue their relationship and that would be a whole lot easier with her in D.C. rather than Iowa.

Except Tiffany had made it clear she wanted nothing to do with the men who lived in D.C. But maybe he'd misunderstood. Maybe she was trying to steer clear of a particular type of man.

"So it's *politicians* in suits who turn you off?" he asked, trying not to give himself away by sounding too hopeful. But, damn it, he *was* hopeful.

"For a man in jeans," she said, flicking a look at the artfully faded ones he'd bought that afternoon, "you seem awfully interested in my views on men in suits."

"I'm interested in how your mind works, that's all," he said, then pressed. "So tell me. Is it politicians you object to?"

She bit her bottom lip as though figuring out how to answer, then got up and walked to the refrigerator. She was wearing tailored slacks and a conservative shirt, but moved with such an innate grace she looked sexier than a swimsuit model.

"I'm having a glass of white wine," she said. "Would you like something?"

He was about to ask for scotch but changed his mind. "Beer, if you have it." Beer not only seemed more in line with what the man he was pretending to be would drink, but he was developing a taste for it.

A moment later she set a frothing mug in front of him and sat down with her glass of white wine. She drained half of it before she spoke.

"I don't object to politicians exactly," she said, giving him a little shrug. "Well, maybe I do. But I try not to. Especially because my father's in Congress."

Her father was a congressman? When they'd been in bed, she'd told him her last name was Albright. His mouth dropped open as he put the pieces together.

"You're Bill Albright's daughter."

She looked taken aback. "You've heard of my father?"

Too late, Chance realized his mistake. As a D.C. lawyer, it wouldn't be entirely unexpected for him to be familiar with some members of Congress. But that world should be as foreign to a drifter from the South as grits were to a society party.

"I'm not sure," he said, inwardly cursing himself. "I might have read something about him. You know how some things stick in your mind."

"But there are more than five hundred members in the House of Representatives. Why would you remember the name Bill Albright?"

He remembered because he'd been introduced to Albright at a charity event for the National Symphony Orchestra barely two weeks before. And because, when a co-worker from his law office mentioned that Albright was a leading proponent of family values, the congressman had talked about the subject at length.

"Maybe it's because he has the same first name as my father," Chance said with sudden inspiration.

"Your father's first name is Bill?"

"Yeah." Chance nodded vigorously although William McMann would probably skewer anyone who dared shorten his name.

"Bill isn't an unusual name," she pointed out.

"No, it's not," he agreed. "So what were you saying about politicians?"

She hesitated, then finally answered. "I was going to say I've been in D.C. long enough to know how politics—and politicians—work."

"What do you mean?" he asked while his impression of her shifted. No wonder he'd sensed she wasn't the classic good-time girl. She not only stuck up for milk and cheese, she was also the daughter of one of congress's most wholesome members.

"Part of it is the you-scratch-my-back-and-I'll-scratch-yours mentality," she said. "You know. I do you a favor and you do one back for me."

Like the favor Chance was doing for Congressman Greeley. His father hadn't specifically said so, but Chance sensed that William McMann had asked him to take this trip to Savannah so he could pay back the congressman for a past favor.

The senior partner of Chance's law firm hadn't been as oblique about his reasons. He'd baldly stated that the firm might need something from Congressman Greeley in the future.

"I guess politicians are like that," he said, mainly because she seemed to be waiting for him to respond.

"It's not only politicians," she said. "It's people in Washington. It's how they operate."

"It couldn't be everybody," he objected.

"Oh, yes. It could," she said. "Believe me, I've been

to enough Washington parties to know. Politicians, bureaucrats, lawyers. They're all the same.''

"Lawyers," he repeated. "I don't think lawyers are like politicians."

"Are you kidding? Image is more important to them than substance. Why do you think so many of them go into politics?"

"That's unfair."

She shook her head. "It's not. When a man asks me out, I'm never sure if it's because he likes me or because he thinks dating Bill Albright's daughter will make him look good."

Chance frowned. "I can't imagine any man having an ulterior motive for dating you." He paused. "Besides getting you into bed."

She rolled her eyes but still smiled. "That's why I approached you on the street, Chance. Because you're not like the men I usually meet."

No, he thought guiltily. He was worse.

"You don't care what people think of you," she continued. "If you did, you wouldn't have sung karaoke tonight. Or worn those tacky clothes the last tenant left behind. Or crashed that party."

He felt like he'd been doused with a torrent of frigid water and it wasn't only because of the bag of ice he was holding against his eye. He'd done all those things because he cared what *she* thought of him.

"That's why I like you," she said, reaching out to touch his cheek. He couldn't help covering her hand with his, even though he didn't deserve her praise. "You are so not like the men I know."

He wouldn't get a better cue to tell her he was exactly like the men she knew. Perhaps he was even worse. He took the ice from his eye, then made the mistake of studying her.

How could he make that confession when she had that soft expression on her face? That spark of warmth in her eyes?

"If the men you know don't appreciate you for who you are, they're idiots," he said.

She laughed. "I'll miss you when you go, Chance McMann."

Their eyes met and the laughter went out of hers. When she spoke, she seemed to make an effort to keep her voice light. "I've been meaning to ask you. When, exactly, will that be?"

"It depends." The next question escaped before he considered what he wanted to say. "How long will you be in town?"

"Until Wednesday."

It was Saturday night. The responsible thing would be to conclude his business tomorrow so he could be back in his office Monday morning.

Except for once in his life, Chance couldn't make himself do the responsible thing. "Then I'll be in town until Wednesday, too," he said.

Her smile was the only reward he needed to tell him the impulsive, irresponsible answer had also been the right one.

He tried not to let it worry him that his answer had cemented her impression of him as a vagabond with nowhere he needed to be.

"How's the eye?" she asked, with a gleam in hers.

"It still hurts like the devil." Even lifting an eyebrow hurt, but he did it anyway. "Why don't you come over here and take a closer look?"

She didn't hesitate, just pushed back her chair, stood up and took two steps until she was in front of him. She smoothed back his hair, her hands lingering in the thick mass as her eyes locked on his. They seemed to have turned a darker, sultrier shade of brown.

"Why don't I kiss it and make it better?" she said, pressing her lips to his swollen flesh.

Although that slight pressure should have made the ache worse, pleasure, sharp and buoyant, coursed through him.

Then she was in his lap, her hands fisting in his hair, her lips on his, her tongue in his mouth. He kissed her back, his thoughts so scrambled that his only coherent one was that she was perfect for him.

As always, her touch inflamed him, the sensations sharper than any he'd felt before. Drawing back from her mouth, even for an instant, took his entire supply of willpower.

"Want to do it on the kitchen table?" he asked, his breathing harsh, his voice unsteady.

The bald truth was that he was so turned on he doubted he'd last if he had to move more than a foot.

"Yes," she said, and he felt her smile against his mouth.

In that instant, before he reclaimed her mouth and

then her body, he realized he'd do anything to keep her close.

Including, it seemed, hiding the truth about who he really was.

THE RAIN CAME DOWN on Savannah in sheets, drenching a city that had been awash in sunshine and celebration twenty-four hours before.

Normally Tiffany enjoyed a good rain. A storm was nature's way of saying it was time to take a break. Go to the movies. Bake cookies. Read a good book.

But today, the rain was making her miserable. The reason wasn't too hard to figure out.

She and Chance were running in it.

"Isn't this great?" Chance raised his muscular arms to the sky as he ran, lifting his face to the heavens. "Bring it on," he yelled.

Beside him, Tiffany sloshed on down a sidewalk deserted except for the two of them. She wore soggy running shoes and a wet T-shirt that probably provided an excellent view of her sports bra.

She'd had reservations about running in the rain when Chance suggested it that morning, but it had been only sprinkling then.

She hadn't anticipated trudging through a downpour with a man who got off on raindrops.

"Wonder why the streets are so empty," he said, keeping up the stream of conversation he'd started when they left the carriage house.

She didn't think it was much of a mystery. It was raining, for pity's sake.

"I bet running's a great way to get rid of a hang-over."

Was he joking? Did he actually believe the drunken partyers from last night were in any shape to lace on a pair of shoes and hit the water-logged streets?

Did he expect to run into Brad, Pete and the black-haired pixie jogging three abreast?

"Yep," he said. "Sweating off a hangover's proba-bly a great way to go."

Tiffany was too wet from the rain to be able to tell whether she was sweating. She stepped into a puddle and got even wetter.

"Isn't this great?" Chance repeated, sounding awed, as though he'd never done it before.

Tiffany knew better.

Jogging was such a regimented activity that she wouldn't have pegged him as a runner, but he'd be doing more huffing and puffing than talking if he wasn't. The way he was lapping up the rain, he prob-ably waited until the skies opened up before he ven-tured out the door.

She managed a noncommittal grunt.

He sent her a concerned look. "Do you want to stop?"

Was he kidding? No way was she prolonging the agony when they'd passed the halfway point a few minutes ago and were headed for home.

"Of course. Not," she said between breaths.

"We could slow down."

"No," she protested loudly, then caught herself. "I mean. No thanks. I run. All. The. Time."

She did, too. Only her runs were of a tamer variety as she joined Washington, D.C.'s exercise-conscious during her lunch hour. If it was raining or the weather was lousy, she headed for the gym.

She reflexively shut her eyes at the rain that sprayed up at her from another of the puddles she and Chance splashed through. She clipped the end of a branch from an overhanging tree and more water hit her with a wet slap.

This is why God invented indoor tracks, she thought.

"You're not much for talking when you run, are you?" he asked as they jogged on.

"Sure. I. Am."

"You are?" He sounded surprised, probably because of her monosyllabic responses. The truth was that talking seriously messed up her breathing patterns.

But now that she'd claimed to like to run and talk at the same time, she had to say something. She remembered committing to happy hour.

"Susie ran into. Friends of ours. Who want to meet. For drinks today," she said, making a concerted effort to get out more than one word at a time. "Want to come?"

"When?" he asked.

"Happy hour. Tonight."

"Love to, but I can't," he said. "I have something I need to do."

She waited for him to explain, but he didn't. Just as he hadn't explained yesterday when she'd driven herself crazy with thoughts of where he was and what he could be doing.

"Is it business?" she ventured.

"It's just something I need to do."

She told herself the way he'd evaded her question didn't matter. Nothing mattered except her deep-seeded belief that he was a good man.

But she couldn't help it. She wanted to know more about him, starting with exactly why he was in Savannah.

Except he wasn't going to tell her. She didn't even know why he was a Southerner without a Southern accent.

They ran on for another minute in silence, through the edge of a tourist district that might have resembled a ghost town if not for the smattering of restaurants open for breakfast.

"There's something else I need to do," Chance said finally, breaking into her despondence.

She slanted him a sidelong look. "What?"

He sped up, executed a quick one-hundred-eighty-degree turn and caught her in his arms before she could stop her forward progress.

"This," he said and kissed her.

His body was slick against hers and the rain was cool as it pelted them, but his mouth was pure heat.

The sensation, she thought numbly, was nearly the same as it had been in the frigid ocean. Heat flared inside of her while her exterior remained cool.

The kiss was out of control from the start, possibly because they were already out of breath from the run.

She spiked her fingers into his wet hair, breathing in the scent of rainwater and man as she kissed him back.

Everything disappeared. The rain. The city. The doubts. Everything but the man.

The kiss went on and on until, finally, they drew back. She could see the strain of restraint on his face and managed to give him a shaky smile because she felt the same.

Had she really lost control that way, on a city street in full view of anyone who happened to glance their way? She consoled herself with the knowledge that the rain had kept most people indoors but her face flamed when her peripheral vision picked up a middle-aged couple sharing a large black umbrella.

She and Chance moved to give them room to maneuver around them on the sidewalk, but the woman stopped dead.

"Oh, my heavens," the woman said, addressing the man. "I was right. It is Elizabeth and William McMann's son."

CHANCE'S STOMACH SANK to his knees as he recognized Helen Toler and her husband Harry. The couple appeared as though they were fresh from Sunday services.

Harry wore an expertly cut dark suit that disguised his thickening middle and spreading behind. Helen looked aristocratic in a chic black skirt and crisp white jacket with her frosted blond hair swept into an artful bun.

Of all of his family's acquaintances, Mrs. Toler was the last one he'd want to witness him kissing a beautiful woman on a rain-soaked day.

But Chance did what everybody who came in contact with Helen Toler did. He grinned and bore it, largely because standing next to her was the president and chief executive officer of the Atlanta Medical University.

Not to mention the man his father had contacted first when Chance's brother Drew was due to graduate from med school and needed a job.

"Hello, Mrs. Toler, Mr. Toler." He dropped his arms from around Tiffany but kept a hand at the small of her very wet back. "This is Tiffany Albright."

He nodded from Tiffany to the Tolers. "Tiffany, meet Helen and Harry Toler."

The rain, blast it, suddenly slowed, making it more feasible to have a conversation.

Chance forced himself to smile, hoping the famously outspoken Helen didn't ask how his law firm in D.C. was treating him. Harry Toler took the wet hand Tiffany offered, but Helen was too busy staring at Chance to notice.

"Why, you've got a black eye," she exclaimed. "However did that happen?"

He was about to dodge the question when Tiffany jumped to his defense. "He got caught in the middle of a fight on River Street last night."

"You were in a street brawl?" Helen appeared mortified.

"He was trying to break it up," Tiffany explained helpfully.

"Doesn't look too bad. Nothing you'd have to trouble your brother with if he'd been in town," Harry said. "How is Drew anyhow? I haven't seen much of him since he went into practice for himself last year."

"He's doing great," Chance said while he tried to think of a way to get away from the couple before they said too much. "Keeping busy."

"He's turned into a fine surgeon, Drew has," Harry said. "Hell, I'd trust him with *my* heart."

During their brief exchange, Helen's horror-rich expression hadn't changed.

"This is such a surprise," she said, her eyes darting from Chance to Tiffany with obvious purpose. Chance felt a trickle of rain drip from his chin and plop to the sidewalk. "Whatever are the two of you doing out in this storm?"

One of the answers was obvious so Chance chose the other.

"We were running, Mrs. Toler."

"Running? In a downpour?"

"It's very refreshing," Chance said, then changed the subject before she could ask another question. "What are you two doing in Savannah?"

"We came for the parade," Harry Toler said.

"We won't be coming again," Helen Toler added. "There was entirely too much revelry."

Chance kept the smile pasted on his face. He'd grown up in Atlanta, only two hundred or so miles west of Savannah. Why hadn't he considered the possibility he'd run into someone he knew?

"I'm surprised to see you here, son," Harry Toler said. A distinguished gentleman in his late fifties, he was as soft spoken as his wife was forceful. "I heard from your father that you'd moved to—"

"I did move, sir," Chance interrupted. "My father was right about that."

"Why a young man like you with a family like that would move away from Atlanta is beyond me," Helen Toler said. "Didn't you take a job with—"

Chance couldn't let her finish. "Excuse me for interrupting, ma'am, but Tiffany and I have to, well, run. We're, um, overheated." He grimaced when he realized what he'd implied. "I mean, we're hot."

Helen Toler gasped.

"I mean, from the rain. And it's not good to stand around in the rain when you're..."

"Hot," Harry Toler supplied, a barely perceptible grin curving his lips. "We understand that. Don't we, dear?"

"But I wanted to ask—"

"Thanks for understanding," Chance said, already ushering Tiffany away. "It was nice seeing you."

"Nice meeting you," Tiffany called but she had to offer the words over her shoulder because Chance was already heading away from the couple at a dead run.

"I take it they're not your favorite people," Tiffany said when they were out of earshot.

"Do you blame me?" Chance asked. "Considering what they interrupted?"

He intended the comment to prevent her from asking how he was acquainted with the Tolers but discovered he'd spoken the truth. He couldn't have known if his heart was pounding like a bongo drum because the Tolers had nearly exposed him or because of that kiss in the rain.

"They didn't interrupt anything," she said, and her breaths once again came in short gasps. "We. Were finished."

"We could have started again."

"Seriously, Chance," she said. "It seemed. As though. You couldn't get. Away from them. Fast enough."

"I couldn't. Harry Toler's a good guy but his wife can be a bit much," he said. "And I was serious. We could have started again. Kissing, I mean."

She didn't say anything for a full minute and he became aware once again of the rhythm of her breathing as she ran. The rain had all but stopped, but drops of moisture still fell on them from the overhanging branches of the city's canopy of trees.

They didn't speak again until they agreed on a mutual stopping place about a quarter of a mile from the carriage house so they had time to cool down.

"You know, you don't have to be ashamed," Tiffany said softly after her breathing had returned to normal.

Chance was walking with his hands on his hips, letting his heartbeat slow. Now it sped up again.

"Of what?"

"Of who you are. Of the kinds of choices you make," she said, her attention fully on him. "I realize your mother's a judge and your brother's a heart surgeon. But you're living the way you want to live. Doing things your way. There's a lot to admire about that."

It hit him that she thought he'd not so subtly disengaged themselves from the Tolers because he didn't want to discuss his lifestyle choices.

Although that was true, she'd misinterpreted the reason.

"I'm not ashamed," he said, then wondered if that was a lie. If he was so comfortable with his choices, why hadn't he told her what they were?

"I can't say the same thing," she said.

"What do you mean?"

"I've never been sure why I became a lobbyist."

"You didn't set out to become one?"

She shook her head. "I didn't have a clear idea of what I wanted to do after college. Then I ran into the president of the dairy council at a party. He offered me a job, which was a little odd because I was an English major. I soon figured out it was because he wanted my father as an ally."

"Then why'd you take the job?"

She worried her lower lip before she answered. "It seemed to make sense at the time. Politics was the world I knew. And it wasn't unethical. I mean, my father would be a proponent of dairy even if I didn't work for the council. But now I think I took the job because I was afraid to try something new."

He put a hand on her back, wanting to comfort her, because he understood what it was to lack courage. He would have chosen to work in a district attorney's office, on the side of the victims, if his father hadn't pushed him into corporate law. But the one time he'd dared mention it, William McMann had shot down the idea like one of the clay pigeons at the skeet range.

"There's no money in it," his father had said. "Don't waste your time."

The salary hadn't mattered to Chance, but he had cared about disappointing his father. So he'd never mentioned working in a D.A.'s office again.

"You did exactly what you wanted to do," Tiffany continued. "That takes courage."

"I'm not who you think I am," he said.

She linked her elbow through his and gave him that smile that usually warmed his heart. Today, it made him feel undeserving.

"I like who you are," she said.

That was the problem. He wasn't anything like the man she thought he was. She stopped walking, stroked his cheek and looked him straight in the eyes.

"I *really* like who you are," she said and pressed her mouth to his.

The familiar sensations humbled him. He didn't deserve her praise. Hell, he didn't deserve her. But he was powerless to keep from wanting her, to keep from reaching for her.

"What do you say we conserve water," she

breathed against his mouth. "Take a shower to-gether?"

"Yes," he said.

He was helpless to make any other reply, but he was equally ineffective against the guilt that rained down on him like the storm that had just ended.

10

"I CAN'T GET OVER HOW MUCH the two of you haven't changed," Rachel Greenburg said, shaking her round, friendly face as she gazed from Tiffany to Susie.

"Especially you, Tiffany," added the redhead perched on the bar stool next to Rachel. Tiffany wished she could remember her name, but they'd run in different circles in high school and nobody had thought to reintroduce them.

She stretched her memory. She thought the woman's mother, or possibly her father, held some important government position. But that hadn't been unusual at Merrifield Academy, where the privileged residents of D.C. schooled their children.

The redhead popped the olive from her drink straw into her mouth. "I swear, it's like you stepped straight from the pages of the yearbook."

Tiffany gritted her teeth in what could have passed for a smile, which was the expression she'd worn since she and Susie had arrived for happy hour. The place was too slick for Tiffany's taste, which led her to believe the redhead had suggested it.

She shifted uncomfortably on her bar stool and made a conscious effort to ease the grip she had on her glass.

"I'm not sure what you mean," Tiffany said.

The redhead smiled at the young, good-looking bartender who winked at her before pouring a drink for another customer. Then she turned her carefully made-up eyes on Tiffany.

"I mean you're still that same sweet girl you were in high school," she answered.

"How do you know she's still sweet?" asked Susie, who was sitting at an angle from them at the corner of the bar. Her expression had a devilish quality as she fished a pretzel from a small bowl. "Maybe she's soured."

"Oh, no." Rachel shook her head vehemently. "Remember when I had that crush on the quarterback? She went up to him for me and asked if he liked me."

"Didn't he say no?" the redhead asked.

"Well, yeah. But it was still a sweet thing to do," Rachel declared. "A person like that doesn't sour."

"Besides, she's drinking ginger ale at happy hour," the redhead said, pointing at Tiffany with a finger decorated with a cherry-red nail.

Tiffany frowned down at her drink, then back up at the redhead. Her eyebrows didn't match the exquisite golden red shade of her hair, which meant the color probably wasn't natural. Somehow, that made Tiffany feel better.

"I drink alcohol," she said. Rarely, but she did.

"It's not only the ginger ale, sweetie. Your hair and makeup make you look sweet, too. But not nearly as much as your clothes."

Tiffany glanced down at the pale blue top she'd

paired with black slacks, which she thought was perfect for happy hour. What was wrong with her outfit?

"I think Tiffany looks nice," Rachel said, and Susie
nodded.

"Of course she does. That's my point. She has the
kind of figure most girls would flaunt but instead she
wears *nice* clothes."

"What's wrong with nice clothes?" Susie asked.

"Nothing. As long as they work with the image
you're trying to project." The redhead caught the bartender's eye and blew him a kiss. "Tiffany's obviously
shooting for...wholesome."

Tiffany noticed the way the other woman paused
before coming up with the description, probably because she didn't use the word often. What woman
who wore a red, strapless minidress to Sunday-night
happy hour did?

"Wholesome," Tiffany repeated, not liking the
sound of the word. "What gives you the impression
that I'm wholesome?"

"I think wholesomeness is a good thing," Rachel
cut in. "Look how far it got Donny and Marie Os-
mond."

"I didn't say it was negative," the redhead said,
sighing loudly. "It was merely an observation. God,
you said you worked for the dairy council. If telling
people to drink milk isn't wholesome, what is?"

"My job's more complicated than that," Tiffany
said. "I help create a successful business climate for
Iowa dairy farmers by lobbying for things like federal
subsidies and money for agriculture projects."

"You're the champion of milk, cheese and yogurt." Rachel beamed at her, the deep lines at the corner of her mouth revealing that she smiled often. "You can't get much more wholesome than that."

"My tourism job's pretty wholesome, too," Susie piped up. "Most people do wholesome things for a living."

"I teach yoga," Rachel said.

The redhead traced the lip of her martini glass with a forefinger. "I get wealthy men to part with their money."

Tiffany couldn't keep the shock off her face. "You what?"

"She's teasing you," Rachel said, shaking her head at the other woman in disapproval. "She works for a yacht brokerage."

"Yes, but my boss only hires female salespeople. He says sex sells, not that we offer it to close the deals." She paused. "Unless the man's really rich and really good-looking."

"You're kidding," Tiffany said.

"Oops." The redhead covered her mouth, then withdrew her hand. "Sorry about that. I didn't mean to shock you."

"Yes, you did. I swear, sometimes I wonder why we ever became friends in the first place," Rachel said, pursing her lips at the other woman. "Considering the things you're saying, it's no wonder Tiffany's surprised."

"What's so surprising about wanting to go to bed with a handsome man? It happens to me all the time."

"All the time?" Susie asked. She was clearly enjoying the outrageous things the redhead was saying. But then, nobody had called *her* wholesome. "When was the last time you saw a man you wanted to go to bed with?"

"You mean besides Artie the bartender over there?" She nodded at the good-looking young man, gave him a finger wave, then paused to consider the question. "Yesterday."

Rachel sat up straighter. "How come you didn't tell me about this?"

The redhead laid a hand on Rachel's shoulder. "There's nothing to tell. Yet. This guy's handsome in that button-down kind of way that makes you want to rip off his suit to get to what's underneath. He comes from money, too, and rich never hurts."

"Rich doesn't matter to me," Tiffany said, her thoughts on Chance. He might not even have a bank account, as far as she knew.

"Do you mean rich doesn't matter to you at all? Or that it wouldn't matter if you were picking up a man for the night?" The redhead took a swallow from her drink. "Not that you would."

Tiffany felt herself bristling. "What makes you think I don't pick up men?"

"Don't let her bait you, Tiffany," Rachel said. "I don't pick up men for wild sex, either."

"I picked up a man this weekend," Tiffany announced. She wished the words back as soon as they were out, but it was too late.

"What did you do with him, sugar?" The redhead

crossed a shapely leg over the other. "Bake him some cookies and give him milk to wash them down with?"

"For your information, she slept with him," Susie proclaimed before Tiffany could say what she'd done with Chance was nobody's business.

"Good for you." The redhead beamed at her and clapped her hands. "Maybe I misjudged you. I never figured you for the type to go in for casual sex."

Tiffany's stomach rolled queasily at her comment. "I wouldn't put it quite that way."

"I would," Susie declared, then gave Tiffany a thumbs-up. "She's not only having casual sex, but lots and lots of it."

"Well then, Tiff, you made my point for me," the redhead said. "We're living in the twenty-first century, thank the Lord. Sex with a handsome man doesn't have to mean anything."

Something inside Tiffany rebelled at her comment, but it was Susie who spoke. "Doesn't it ever mean anything to you?"

"She says she's not looking for meaningful," Rachel supplied, shaking her head. "She says she'll settle down some day but for now she just wants to have fun."

"But what about love?" Tiffany blurted out.

"Love?" The redhead sounded incredulous. "What's love got to do with it?"

"These men you sleep with," Tiffany said slowly, "isn't there a chance you'll fall in love with one of them?"

"That's about as likely as you falling in love with

the guy you picked up." The redhead let out a disbelieving snort. "The kind of sex you have with guys like that doesn't mean anything. It's just sex."

"I suppose," Tiffany muttered, but her lower lip trembled so much she had to bring her glass to her mouth to hide it.

"Oh, honey," Rachel said, reaching across the counter to pat her free hand. "You haven't fallen for the guy you picked up, have you?"

"That's a cardinal sin," the redhead added.

"Of course I haven't fallen for him," Tiffany said with a tight smile. "It's just that I, um, remembered I was supposed to call him. Let him know where we could meet later. Could you excuse me for a minute?"

"Do you want me to come with you?" Susie asked as an indentation appeared between her eyebrows.

"Of course not. I'll be right back." Tiffany got off the bar stool and backed away before Susie could protest further. "I'll be able to hear better on my cell phone in the lobby. I won't be long."

A minute later, Tiffany leaned with her back against one of the marbled walls in a far corner of the lobby.

She and Chance were supposed to meet later at the carriage house so there was no need to call him. What she needed was to get a grip.

She should be thanking her ex-classmate for opening her eyes instead of shaking over the implications of what she'd said.

Of course what she and Chance had was temporary.

She liked and admired him but she'd be delusional

to believe they had a future together. Even if he asked, did she really believe she could give up a good job and a stable existence to live like a gypsy with Chance?

She didn't even like songs about gypsies. She cringed every time "Gypsies, Tramps and Thieves" came on the radio.

What she needed, she thought as she wiped some moisture from her cheek, was to stop taking everything so seriously.

She straightened from the wall, squared her shoulders, and froze at the sight of the gorgeous, brown-haired man striding through the lobby toward the exit. In blue jeans and a pale denim shirt, he commanded more attention than any of the better dressed men in the hotel. Even if he did have a black eye. But what was he doing here?

"Chance," she called, intending to find out.

AT THE SOUND OF HIS NAME, Chance pivoted to see Tiffany gaping at him from the far end of the lobby.

With her long, silky hair tumbling about her shoulders and her baby-doll mouth parted in surprise, she looked like a vision. His heart gave a wild leap of joy until he realized their accidental meeting wasn't necessarily a positive thing.

"Tiffany." He took a sharp right turn and headed toward her as his mind whirred. What was she doing here? More important, how could he explain why he was inside one of Savannah's priciest hotels? "I thought you were meeting Susie and some other friends for happy hour."

"I am." She nodded toward the lounge where he and Mary Greeley had gotten together only yesterday. "I came outside for some air. Why are you here?"

I was using my hotel room to change out of my suit so you don't realize how unsuitable I am for you, he thought.

He bent to kiss her swiftly on the mouth only partly to give him time to think how to answer. Just like that, his heart sped up.

He drew back, noticing that every inch of her was perfectly turned out. He'd liked her better wet, naked and streaming with water. The way she had been when they'd made love in the shower that morning.

"Chance," she repeated, her lips so soft and dewy he was tempted to dive in for another kiss. She caught her lower lip with her upper teeth and his gut clenched. "You still haven't told me what you're doing here."

"Meeting you," he said on a burst of inspiration. With his blood rushing from his head to various other parts of him, it was a wonder he could think at all. "The thing I had fell through so I thought I'd join you for drinks."

At least that was the partial truth. The woman threatening to sue Mary Greeley had left word at the hotel desk that she was in too much pain to meet today and rescheduled for tomorrow.

A ploy, to be sure, but the postponement had given Chance a legitimate explanation for why he was extending his business trip when he'd checked in with his father that afternoon.

"I don't remember telling you where we were meeting," Tiffany said as lines appeared on her forehead.

"You must have."

"Why's that?" She looked even more puzzled.

"Why else would I be here?" he asked, shoving aside the guilt.

"But I could have sworn you were walking out of the hotel instead of into it."

"I didn't see you in the bar so I *was* leaving," Chance said, figuring he better change the subject. "Does the offer of drinks still stand?"

She stared at him for a minute, probably wondering why she hadn't seen him check the bar when she was standing in the lobby. For just an instance, he thought about coming clean.

But then her dark eyes cleared and she touched his cheek. Warmth from her hand spread to every part of him.

"Of course the offer stands," she said softly, but she didn't remove her hand. Instead she dropped it and traced his bottom lip with her forefinger.

"If you don't stop looking at me like that," he said thickly, "I won't be in any shape to meet Susie and your other friends."

He saw resignation in her eyes before she took his hand and led him toward the lounge. Steps from the entrance, she suddenly stopped.

"One of the women in there isn't exactly my friend," she said. "She'll probably take one look at you and salivate."

"Or run away," he said, pointing to the discoloration around his eye.

She shook her head. "Believe me. This woman wouldn't run."

"Then I would," he said, looking her directly in the eyes, "straight to you."

Her face creased into a beautiful smile that reached her dark eyes, then she winked at him and squeezed his hand before letting it go. "Hold that thought and wait here."

He watched her flag down the nearest cocktail waitress, bend over to whisper something in her ear and then nearly sprint to the front desk on legs he knew were long and beautiful beneath her slacks.

"I'll just be a minute," she called to him as she passed.

He followed her and stood back to watch while she talked to a desk clerk, wondering what she was up to. He had a pretty good guess minutes later when she walked back to where he was standing, a wicked smile wreathing her face.

"I'm getting the feeling you told that waitress to let your friends know we're not meeting them," he said in a low voice. "Am I right?"

She nodded, her eyes on his lips. "I have something more...enjoyable in mind."

He swallowed, intending to ask her to elaborate,

but his throat felt too thick to speak. Her dark eyes danced as she held out a computerized key card.

"Hey, lover," she said in a sultry voice. "Want to get lucky?"

TIFFANY PULLED CHANCE into the hotel suite, barely waiting until he'd shut the door behind them before she undid the first button of his denim shirt.

"Talk about luck." His low voice sent shivers tumbling over Tiffany's skin that had nothing to do with the low setting on the room's air conditioner. "This is better than winning the lottery."

"It's about to get even better," she said as she went for another button.

Her senses had come alive the instant she'd spotted him in the lobby. Now her body felt inflamed, as though gripped by a fever.

How could she have doubted what she and Chance had was about sex? That's what she craved, what her body was primed for.

Four of his buttons were unfastened now, baring the muscular beauty of a chest sprinkled with dark hair. She dipped a hand inside his shirt, delighting in the feel of warm skin, hard muscle and rough hair against her fingertips, reveling in the way he sucked in a sharp breath.

But it wasn't enough. She wanted more of his skin exposed.

She pulled his shirt free of his jeans and tore at the rest of the buttons. A few of them popped off and fell with soft plops onto the plush carpeting of the hotel room. His shirt hung open, his chest partially exposed.

"Whoa," he said thickly as she slipped the shirt from his body. "We've got all night."

She trailed her hands over the solid thickness of his shoulders and the warm naked skin of his back. "Do you really want me to slow down?"

She smoothed both hands over his upper chest, then lightly flicked both nipples with her thumbs before pressing an openmouthed kiss directly over his heart. She felt him grow hard through his jeans and looked up to meet his passion-dazed eyes.

"I thought," she said, pausing to kiss him again before finishing her sentence, "you liked this."

"I do," he said, gasping.

She undid the button at the waistband of his jeans, tugging his zipper down so that he sprang free of the confines. She slid one hand slowly down his body until she was rubbing the hard length of him through his underwear.

"And this?" she breathed as her hand pressed against him. "Do you like this?"

"Oh, yeah," he said on a growl that inflamed her even further. She felt her nipples tighten and liquid pool in her center.

Just sex, the redhead had said.

That's what this was, she told herself as she found the elastic of his Jockey shorts and tugged it downward, pulling off his underwear along with his jeans.

His clothes pooled at his ankles, leaving most of his glorious body naked.

Just sex.

She covered his mouth with hers, thrusting her tongue deep inside as she skimmed her hands down his body, eager to touch every naked inch of his sleek skin.

They were both breathing hard when she surfaced for air but she didn't want to stop for long. She nuzzled his neck and bit him lightly on the earlobe as one of her hands encircled his penis.

Just sex, she mentally repeated to herself as she glided her hand up and down his erection. Her breaths, as well as his, came in rapid pants.

"There's a...perfectly good...bed over there," he said unsteadily.

"Too far," she breathed against his mouth.

"But you're—" he closed his eyes and groaned as she continued to stroke him "—too dressed."

"Not for long," she said, stepping back from him and loosening her blouse from her slacks so she could pull it over her head.

He took the cue and removed his shoes and socks before stepping the rest of the way out of his clothing. Then he waited, watching her undress.

Her hands shook, making it hard to unzip her slacks, causing her to falter when she unclasped the front fastener of her bra. It took three tries for her to shimmy out of her panties.

Just sex, she told herself to explain the shaking.

Finally she stood naked before him. He wet his lips as he stared at her, his eyes darkening with passion.

She knew what he was seeing. Her nipples were

pebbled, her skin flushed, her chest heaving in and out with quick, excited breaths.

Just sex, she told herself again.

Her body was ready for it.

She took a step toward him, intending to continue where she'd left off, but he reached for her before she could touch him. Then he swung her into his arms as though she weighed little more than a rag doll.

"What are you doing?" she asked even as she linked her arms around his neck and snuggled against him. He smelled like rain, she thought absently. Clean and heady, like the storm they'd run in earlier.

He strode through the suite with a quick, sure grace and went through the open door to the bedroom. He pulled back the rich burgundy and green quilt, then laid her almost reverently on the white sheets that covered the king-size bed.

In seconds, he'd stretched out beside her. He rested his weight on one elbow as he peered down into her face.

"As much as I liked what we were doing out there," he said softly, "I want to make love to you properly."

His large, warm hand started at her hip and glided over her stomach before finally stopping at her breast. He caressed and gently squeezed her sensitive flesh, causing heat to shoot to her center. She gasped, closing her eyes at the sharp sensation.

When she opened her eyes, she found that she was looking directly into his.

His face was tight with passion, his skin ruddy with it, but his eyes were soft. The eyes of a lover, not a stranger.

All along she'd been telling herself this was just sex, but he claimed he'd carried her to the bed so they could make love.

"Ah, Tiffany," he said as his hand moved from her breast to her neck and then cupped the back of her head. He looked deep into her eyes. "Can you see what you do to me? Can you feel it?"

His mouth covered hers, cutting off the necessity of a reply. Their bodies met, naked skin to naked skin. She could feel his heart pounding against hers, smell his unique scent, taste the heat of his kiss.

Oh, yes, she knew what she did to him. Because he was doing the same thing to her.

She whimpered deep in her throat when he cupped her breast and his finger circled the nipple. She lifted her hips to press her center against him when she felt the heat of his erection against her body.

She gasped in protest when he lifted his body from hers but soon realized that he was reaching for a condom.

"Hurry," she said.

"Believe me, I am," he said, a spark of passion-dark mischief in his eyes as he sheathed himself. He reached for her again and she pulled the entire length of him against her.

Just sex, she told herself again, as she opened her legs to him and the head of his penis nudged at her opening.

This time she didn't believe it.

She'd had "just sex" before. Pleasant, unspectacular sex that had left her feeling hollow. That hollow feeling was why she didn't make a habit of sleeping around.

Deep in her heart, she'd known there was more to the act than physical gratification. Now, as she welcomed Chance inside her and he made love to her with deep, steady strokes, she realized she had found it.

She and Chance weren't having sex.

They were making love, because she was in love with him.

The knowledge was so earth-shattering that she almost shouted it. But then he thrust into her again and her world came apart.

Waves of sensation roiled through her, so intense that she couldn't speak, could only cry out with senseless sounds of pleasure.

She took him to her hilt, wrapping her legs around his waist and grasping him to her by the sleek skin of his back.

The waves built, transporting her higher and higher, until they came crashing down in an intense wall of feeling. She had her eyes closed but she saw stars, a brilliant array of them that showered down on her like rain.

He cried out a moment later and she felt the shudder of his body as his orgasm came quickly on the heels of hers.

They stayed joined together as their heartbeats slowed and their breathing returned to normal.

Just love, she thought when she could think again.

Another few moments passed before he lifted his

head, smoothed the hair back from her forehead and gave her a heart-melting smile.

"Wow," he said.

Even with his black eye, she thought he was the most beautiful sight she'd ever seen. Her heart turned over.

"You won't get any arguments from me there," she said, reaching up to touch his cheek. "Wow."

He rolled off her but kept his arms around her, bringing her with him so they reversed positions and she was the one lying on top of him. She giggled at the sudden disorientation.

"That's better," he said. "Now I'm not crushing you."

"I like the way you crush," she said, linking her arms around his neck. "I like everything about you."

A shadow seemed to cross over his face. "You don't know everything about me."

"I know that I want you," she said, keeping her eyes locked on his so he knew she was serious. She took a breath for courage and plunged ahead. The knowledge was too powerful, too wonderful to keep to herself. "I know that I love you."

This time she thought she saw joy in his expression but then his brow wrinkled and his eyes grew serious.

"Tiffany," he began. "There are things about me you don't understand."

"I know that," she said, surprised that the things she didn't understand about him no longer ate at her. She knew enough. She knew he was a kind, good man. She knew that she loved him. "I also know you'll tell me about them when you're ready."

He sighed. "Maybe you won't like what I have to say."

"That's another chance I'm willing to take."

He started to interrupt but she covered his lips with her fingers.

"Shhh. Let me finish. I'm not a snob, Chance. So what if you can't settle down in one place. I can live with that."

She tried a smile but felt it waver. He hadn't told her he loved her, hadn't asked her to give up anything for him, but still she needed to make the offer.

"If you want me to," she said softly.

Again, she read uncertainty on his face. She was being too forward, assuming too much, but the fact that she loved him was so overwhelming that she couldn't help it.

"It's okay," she said, her smile wavering. "You don't have to say anything."

"You don't understand. I want to," he said and she heard his sigh with her heart as well as her ears. "I want you."

"Then take me."

She moved sensuously against him and lowered her mouth to his. But before his kiss rendered her powerless to think, she realized that her entire world had changed.

She'd spoken the truth when she told Chance she'd give up her job and her home to be with him.

She wouldn't have to surrender her heart. Because he already had it.

11

CHANCE SAT FULLY DRESSED on the edge of the hotel bed, noting the way the weak light that filtered into the room through a crack in the curtain made Tiffany's sleeping face appear almost ethereal.

He needed to rouse her and tell her he had to leave but instead just sat there, staring at her.

Amazing how someone so full of life and passion, he thought, could look so delicate in sleep.

If he awakened her with a kiss, he had little doubt she'd respond enthusiastically. But he couldn't trust himself to touch her, not when he needed to meet with Mary Greeley and the litigious Betsy Leland in less than forty-five minutes.

He didn't have time to linger in bed with Tiffany. Truth be told, he didn't have time to linger *on* the bed, either. Still, he didn't move.

She'd pulled the sheets up in sleep but one of her creamy shoulders was exposed. Her dark hair fanned the pillow, her face innocent and peaceful. And beautiful. He couldn't forget beautiful.

Last night she'd told him she loved him.

It was too soon, of course. They'd only met days ago, which had been far too little time for her to reach such a momentous conclusion.

He extended his fingers and skimmed them across her check and her eyelids cracked open. She gave him a sleepy, happy smile.

"Good morning," she said.

He'd exercised tremendous restraint in the minutes he'd sat on the bed watching her sleep, but now it broke. He dipped his head and kissed her. Her mouth was soft from sleep, making the kiss all the sweeter.

"Good morning yourself," he said when he raised his head.

He saw his reflection in her smiling eyes and barely recognized himself. Was he really that contented-looking, tousle-haired man with a black eye who needed a shave?

"You look happy," she said.

"I am happy." He spoke nothing but the truth.

"If you stick around, I could make you happier," she said. Her eyes were half-lidded but still he read the invitation in them.

"I have no doubt about that." He cupped her hip over the sheet, not trusting himself to touch any part of her skin that wasn't covered. She purred deep in her throat, sending a shiver of sensation dancing over him. "Believe me, I'd like to stick around. But I can't."

"Why not?"

He hesitated. "I've got a thing I need to do."

"Oh," she said shortly and her eyes shifted away from his.

Last night she'd claimed his secretiveness didn't matter. She'd insisted she didn't need to know any details he wasn't ready to share. The flash of hurt he'd glimpsed in her eyes told him that wasn't true.

"Look, it's after nine now. This shouldn't take long. Why don't I meet you at the carriage house at, say, two?"

"I don't know," she said, her voice sounding thick. "I might, um, be busy."

She was brushing him off, giving him the big sayonara. It was exactly what he deserved, but it still hurt. But how could he blame her? He'd been nothing but evasive from the moment they met, wanting to know about her but sharing little of himself.

The knowledge that he had to tell her everything, no matter what the cost, hit him like a bolt of lightning. A relationship built on evasions and half-truths would fizzle to nothing. He filled his lungs with air and let out a slow breath.

"Listen, Tiffany," he began, "I haven't been completely forthright with you."

"Doesn't matter," she mumbled.

"It does matter," he said, then sighed. "Would you please look at me?"

When she turned the full power of her dark gaze on him, he read distrust in her eyes. His stomach pitched sickeningly.

"I have to..." He'd meant to say he had to leave her bed because he was meeting with a client, but then he'd have to reveal he was an attorney.

That conversation would take longer than the few minutes he had before he needed to head back to his hotel room to shower and change for his fast-approaching meeting with Betsy Leland and Mary Greeley.

"You have to what?" Tiffany asked.

"Leave," he said on a sad sigh. "I have to leave."

Her eyes flicked away from his and her chin quivered. "Whatever," she said.

"You didn't let me finish." He tipped up her chin so she had to look at him. Her eyes didn't look angry, but so sad his heart lurched. "I have to leave *now*. But I have all afternoon free. This afternoon I'll tell you whatever you want to know."

She didn't believe him. He could see it in her guarded expression.

"I don't have a Southern accent because my parents made sure my brother and I didn't pick one up," he blurted out. "They thought an accent might limit the opportunities available to us."

She blinked, but her eyes still looked shuttered. "Why did you tell me that?"

"Because you asked me the other day and I didn't answer." He rubbed his forehead. When he spoke, his voice was urgent. "I guess I wanted to show that you can trust me."

He watched indecision war on her face. He could tell that she wanted to put her faith in him, but she wasn't sure whether she should.

"Trust me," he repeated. "I promise I'll answer all your questions this afternoon. Whatever they are."

She bit her lip as she continued to gaze at him, searching his face for he didn't know what. For a terrible minute, he thought she'd tell him it was already too late. That she was no longer interested in anything he had to say. Finally she spoke.

"What if I ask who your favorite cartoon character is and why?"

He blew out a relieved breath and gave her a shaky smile. "Bugs Bunny. Because he's way smarter than any silly theme-park mouse."

She laughed, and his heart swelled with love for her.

Love.

The same kind she'd talked about the night before. It didn't matter that they barely knew each other, that it was too soon to feel this way. He loved her and knew with a stunning certainty that he'd never love anyone quite the same way again.

I love you, he thought.

But he couldn't say the words, not until she knew the sort of man he really was. Hope surged through him. He'd make her understand she could not only be happy with a Starched Suit but that she belonged with one.

She belonged with him. The man who loved her.

He kissed her again, urgently this time. His body angled over hers, his hands tangling in her hair. He dared not move them southward because then he'd never be on time for his blasted appointment. She twined her arms around his neck and held him close, her tongue meeting his thrust for thrust until he was weak with wanting her.

With a supreme effort, he turned his mouth away

from hers, groaning as she pressed little kisses along his jawline.

"I have to go," he said, needing to hear the words.

Ignoring his body's response, he stood up and gazed down at her. Her face was soft with passion, her cheeks flushed, her dark hair billowing around her face. He reached down to cup her cheek, his gaze on the kiss-swollen lips he already wanted to ravage again.

"This afternoon," he promised. "I'll tell you everything this afternoon."

"I believe you," she said, then paused. "I believe *in* you."

He made himself turn away from the inviting picture she made and head out the hotel room door. It wasn't until he reached the elevator and pressed a button for an upper floor that her words registered.

Would she believe in him if she saw him heading for another hotel room instead of the lobby?

Not only was the bulk of his luggage in that room but so was a duplicate set of toiletries. He'd purchased them so he could keep his worn leather bag at Tiffany's and keep her from finding out anything relevant about him.

He wasn't sure when it had happened but over the past few days he'd begun to actively deceive the woman he loved.

"I'm reprehensible," he said aloud as the elevator door slid open. He didn't notice the elderly woman inside until she backed up flush against the back of the cage. He gave her what he hoped was a reassuring smile.

Her eyes narrowed behind her glasses and she raised the knobby cane she held. "I have a weapon and I know how to use it," she said in a shrill voice.

Before he could respond, she thrust out the cane and jabbed the button for the next floor. He noticed she'd originally planned to travel to a different, higher floor. Oh, brother, was she actually afraid of him?

"I'm not really reprehensible," he said when the elevator began its upward climb. "I'm actually quite respectable."

"Sweet talking me won't work." She held her cane in front of her like a shield. "I heard what I heard."

The elevator jerked to a halt and the woman moved toward the doors, being careful to keep him in her sights. She backed out the elevator and hurried down the hall, sneaking backward looks at him.

He sighed heavily.

This afternoon, when he tried to convince Tiffany to award him a second chance, he'd have to be careful of his editorial comments.

Calling himself reprehensible would definitely not be in his best interest.

THE TEENAGE GIRL WHO PASSED Tiffany in the hotel hallway wore a grimace worthy of a torture victim.

"For your information, it's afternoon," she said testily before covering her ears.

Tiffany wondered what the girl's problem was until

it dawned on her that she was whistling. Okay, she wasn't whistling exactly. More like drawing in breaths that sounded vaguely chirpy.

With a start, she recognized the breaths loosely resembled the tune of "Oh, What a Beautiful Morning."

She immediately stopped whistling, turning to call after the teenager. "Sorry about that, but it is a beautiful day."

The girl's groan was audible from five doors away.

"She must've got up on the wrong side of the bed this morning," Tiffany said to herself. Tiffany most definitely had not, especially because Chance had spent most of the night on the other side of the bed.

Chance.

Could there be a more wonderful man?

Granted, she didn't know much about the mundane details of his life but she did know a beautiful man lived underneath all that gorgeous skin. A man she could trust.

She was surprised to see the elevator door in front of her so soon. It had seemed to take no time at all to walk the length of the hall, almost as though she'd been floating.

Floating while singing, "Oh, What a Beautiful Morning."

She giggled. She really must be in love.

A high-pitched tone signaled that the elevator had stopped on her floor. She waited until the door opened and smiled at the white-haired couple inside the cage. The man stood protectively close to the woman, who leaned heavily on a gnarled cane.

"Good morning," Tiffany said cheerfully.

The man greeted her with a nod but the woman tapped the face of her watch. Tiffany looked at hers, only to discover it was well past noon. She gave the couple an apologetic shrug.

They rode the elevator in silence for a few moments before she became aware of the couple's low-voiced disagreement.

"She's a female riding the elevator alone," she heard the elderly woman say with asperity. "She needs to be told."

"Told what?" Tiffany asked, wondering at the deep lines between the woman's brows and the unhappy slant to her mouth.

"Told about the reprehensible characters riding the elevator," the elderly woman said.

Reprehensible? Now that was a word you didn't hear every day.

Tiffany kept her smile plastered on her face. She doubted that even a hotel full of reprehensible characters could dampen her mood.

When you were in love, few things could.

"A woman alone can't be too careful," the woman called after her when the elevator came to a stop and Tiffany emerged into the lobby.

"I'll remember that," Tiffany said and promptly forgot everything but the rumbling of her stomach.

She hadn't intended to skip breakfast but she'd been so overwhelmingly tired that she'd fallen back asleep almost as soon as Chance had left that morning.

A night of making wild, passionate love tended to tire a person out.

She hadn't eaten anything, in fact, since she and Chance had ordered room service the night before. He'd insisted on champagne with their meal, she remembered as her stomach gave a giddy little jump.

He'd also insisted on paying, making her wonder how he could foot such a hefty bill. She remembered that Helen Toler had implied he had a job. This afternoon, she'd find out exactly where he worked.

But first, she needed food.

The scent of grilling hamburgers stopped her a few feet from the entrance to the hotel restaurant. She exercised regularly and generally watched her diet, but she couldn't resist a good burger.

She raised a hand to check her hair, which she'd washed and blow-dried that morning after showering. As for her clothes, they were the same ones she'd worn the night before but could pass for daytime wear.

If she'd been in Washington, D.C., she'd ignore her growling stomach and go home. But this was Savannah, where she didn't need to be overly concerned with appearances.

She looked presentable enough. It was barely half past noon, which would give her time to grab a quick sandwich and be back at the carriage house by two to meet Chance.

Making up her mind, she crossed to the hostess stand and requested a table for one.

"I DON'T HAVE MUCH TIME," Chance said as he and Mary Greeley settled into a table for two in the hotel restaurant. "I'm meeting someone at two."

"If you don't stop saying you have to leave, my feelings will get hurt." Mary stuck out her lower lip in a pretty pout. Today her hair was a subtle shade of red, making him wonder how often she changed the color. "We're supposed to be celebrating."

Chance personally didn't think there was much to celebrate.

He'd come to Savannah in full agreement with Mary's congressman father that they should offer Betsy Leland a cash payment not to file suit. Chance had changed his mind somewhere along the line, but he hadn't been able to change Jake Greeley's.

Despite Chance's strong opinion that a judge would throw the case out of court for lack of evidence, the congressman had insisted Chance offer cash in return for Leland agreeing in writing not to pursue the lawsuit.

Chance had done as directed, but it galled him that they'd settled a groundless case.

"I suppose you're relieved this is all over," Chance said, trying to find the silver lining in the situation.

Mary leaned back in her chair so that her impressive breasts looked like they might pop through her tight yellow top. "How can I be relieved when I was never worried in the first place?"

Chance's eyebrows rose. "You weren't afraid the newspapers would get hold of the story?"

The congressman's theory had been that if the case

landed on a court docket a reporter might pick up the story, complete with Betsy Leland's claim that his daughter had been drinking and driving.

"Daddy was afraid of publicity, not me." Mary made a face. "Don't tell me you didn't figure out this was all about Daddy? When your father is a congressman, most things are."

"Maybe you're being too hard on your father," Chance said. "I'm sure he was thinking about preserving your reputation."

"Oh, please," Mary said with a husky laugh. She leaned forward so that he had an excellent view of her cleavage. "Daddy's a politician. It's his own reputation he's worried about. Besides, I don't worry about mine so why should he? Everybody who knows me knows I'm no choir girl."

She licked her lips with a sensuous slide of her tongue and reached across the table to walk her fingers up his arm.

"Would you like to get to know me better, Chauncy?" she asked, her voice a throaty purr.

He nearly swatted her hand away but figured that wasn't the most diplomatic way to convey the message that he wasn't interested.

He leaned toward her, intending to let her down easily. A hostess carrying a menu walked briskly by their table, but no customer followed her.

"Oh, my gosh," came a voice from behind him. "Isn't this a coincidence?"

Chance's stomach clenched as he recognized the voice. It was the same one that had whispered words of love to him during the most spectacular night of his life.

He prepared to turn around, wondering how she had recognized him when his back was to her.

"Oh, hello, Tiffany," Mary said before he had the chance. "Fancy meeting you here."

12

MARY GREELEY.

That was the redhead's name, Tiffany thought triumphantly as she nodded at the woman she'd met for happy hour the night before.

It was all coming back to her now. Mary was congressman Jake Greeley's daughter. She'd been a blonde in high school, which must have been one of the reasons Tiffany had trouble remembering her.

"Wherever did you get off to last night?" Mary asked, gazing at her over her dining companion's very broad shoulder.

"Something came up," Tiffany said.

"I can understand that." Mary let her gaze roam over the man at her table. "If I'm not mistaken, something was about to come up for me, too."

The sexual implication in her comment was unmistakable, making Tiffany curious to get a look at her latest victim.

"Where are my manners?" Mary pointed at the man with a long-nailed flourish. "Tiffany, I'd like you to meet my lawyer, Chauncy McMann."

It took so long for the man to turn that Tiffany felt as though he was moving in slow motion, like a scene in an old movie. The surreal feeling continued when she found herself staring at Chance.

She shook her head, refusing to believe her eyes.

Chance wasn't a lawyer any more than he was a Starched Suit. He wouldn't be sitting in a restaurant dressed in an expensive-looking cream-colored ensemble and answering to the name of Chauncy.

He especially wouldn't be sitting in a restaurant with Mary, who'd all but stated he would be her next course.

"Tiffany, I can explain," the man in the suit said in an urgent voice.

The synapses between her eyes and brain snapped together, giving her no choice but to believe what was in front of her.

The man she'd told she loved less than twenty-four hours before was a Starched Suit. A lying, cheating one at that.

"You two know each other?" Mary asked. "Oh, right. It's the D.C. connection. How could I forget how closely law is tied to politics?"

"Politics?" Tiffany managed to croak.

"I'm sure Chance knows how important it is for lawyers to associate with politicians and lobbyists," Mary said. "Why else would he be handling this case for my father?"

"I'm handling the case because our fathers are friends," Chance stated firmly.

"And because Daddy's an influential man."

The guilty look on Chance's face told Tiffany more clearly than words that Mary had hit the mark. She stared at him, feeling her blood drain until it took an effort to stand.

She'd thought he was a nomadic good-time guy when all the while he was exactly what she'd been trying to escape: A D.C. Starched Suit who moved in the political world.

How he must have been laughing at her.

"The tension's so thick I'm thinking about picking up my butter knife," Mary said, looking from Chance to Tiffany. "If one of you doesn't quick tell me what's going on, I'll die on the spot of curiosity."

"Ma'am, I lost you on the way to the table." The hostess must have doubled back when she realized Tiffany hadn't followed her. She seemed to change what she was about to say in midsentence. "Is something wrong?"

"Yes," Tiffany said.

She backed up a step, her chest heaving so hard it hurt to breathe. Then she pivoted and rushed for the restaurant exit, weaving through tables and past surprised diners.

"Tiffany, wait. We need to talk," Chance called after her but she dared not slow down, especially because she was sure he was giving chase.

Her mind ran over the events of the last few days, pausing at any number of times he could have told her who he was.

It was too late for talking now.

"Tiffany!"

Chance's voice chased her into the beautifully decorated lobby while her options ran through her mind.

She could head for the street but then he would most certainly catch up to her. The elevator wasn't a possibility for the same reason. He'd slip inside before she could escape.

Where could she go that he wouldn't dare follow?

Her gaze snagged on the rest rooms at the opposite side of the lobby and she made up her mind. She dashed for a door, yanked it open and rushed inside.

At the sight of a short, middle-aged man at the sink washing his hands, she skidded to a stop. He caught her eyes in the mirror and snorted, shaking his graying head.

"I don't care if the ladies' room is too crowded," he said tiredly, "you women do not have the right to barge into the men's room."

The men's room?

A quick glance around revealed a row of urinals against the wall. She was in the men's room all right.

While she digested that fact, the disgruntled man headed for the door. He was almost there when it burst open. Chance bumped into him with such an impact that Tiffany thought he'd topple like a bowling pin. But then Chance reached out and caught him.

"Sorry, buddy," he said, but his eyes were on Tiffany.

She backed away from him, closer to the urinals.

"What is it with you people?" the man said testily.

"He said he was sorry," Tiffany pointed out, then could have kicked herself. Why was she sticking up for a traitor like Chance? "Forget I said that. Yell at him all you like."

"You're the one who should be yelled at," the man admonished.

"Hey," Chance said, his chest puffing out. "Don't talk to her like that."

"I don't particularly want to talk to either one of you," the man said with a huff before he marched for the exit.

Tiffany didn't watch him go. She was too busy weighing her chances of making a break for the door. Considering the six feet of determined man standing in the way, she concluded they were dim.

"Get out of here," she said, her breathing uneven from her recent exertion. She wouldn't consider the possibility it was because of Chance, because this wasn't him.

The Chance she'd come to love dressed in T-shirts and blue jeans and had a fun-loving manner that surrounded him like air. Aside from the black eye, this man could have been lifted straight from the sterile pages of an upscale men's fashion magazine.

He wore pants with razor-sharp creases, a crisp pin-striped shirt and a silk tie in a muted pattern. The jacket that covered his broad shoulders fit perfectly, with none of the bumpy pockets of material common to less expensive suits.

Add a smoothly shaved face and a well-groomed head of dark hair and he looked like a stranger.

"You're the one in the men's room," he pointed out.

"Only because I thought it was the ladies' room," she said. "I was trying to get away from you."

"Wouldn't have worked," he said, shaking his head

so his dark hair rustled. "I'd have followed you any-where."

He looked serious, earnest and unfamiliar. She had to remember the last one.

"Why bother?" she asked, then made a show of tap-ping her chin. "Oh, I get it. One woman isn't enough for you. When you're through with Mary, you want to have another one lined up."

Chance let out a disbelieving snort. "You can't pos-sibly believe I have something going with a client."

She didn't believe that and only partly because Mary's prerequisites for coming on to a man seemed to be that he was breathing. She wouldn't have be-lieved it even if Mary hadn't been his client.

"I know what you think you saw but that's not how it is." Chance released a short breath. "I admit Mary propositioned me, but I was thinking of a way to let her down easy."

She shuffled her feet, staring at the floor, not want-ing to give him the satisfaction of admitting she bought his story. Neither did she care to examine the reasons for her bone-deep certainty that Chance wasn't carrying on with Mary.

"Why should I believe you?" she asked.

"Because it's the truth."

"And you're big on truth, right?" she asked sarcas-tically.

He winced. "I deserved that, but how can you think I'd look at another woman after last night?"

The reminder of what they'd shared sent a shard of

pain shooting through Tiffany. She raised angry eyes to his.

It was time to stop pretending this was about Mary.

"I didn't even know who I was sleeping with last night," she bit out.

He sighed and rubbed a hand over his lower jaw. He looked so unhappy that she felt a pang of sympathy for him, which she ruthlessly quashed.

"I never lied to you about who I was. My name *is* Chance McMann."

"*Chauncy* McMann," she said, using a haughty voice to put the emphasis on his first name.

"Everybody but my father and the occasional client calls me Chance."

"Chauncy suits a fancy lawyer like you better. Is that why you never mentioned your birth name?"

"Of course not," Chance said. "I never mentioned it because it wasn't important."

"So it wasn't important to tell me what you did for a living or where you lived, either?"

"You didn't ask me where I worked," he pointed out. "You were the one who never wanted details. You wanted to keep things secret."

"And you took that as permission to let me believe you were a drifter? Tell me something, *Chauncy*. Has this footloose and fancy-free act of yours worked on women before?"

He recoiled as if she'd struck him. "That's not fair. I never told you that. You reached your own conclusions."

"Conclusions you didn't bother correcting. God, I

should have guessed it. I knew your mother was a judge, that your brother was a surgeon. Tell me, what does your father do?"

Chance hesitated. "He's an attorney, too."

It was all too much. Her lower lip started to tremble and she mercilessly caught it between her teeth. He took a step toward her, and she took a step back.

"Don't cry, Tiffany," he said softly. "I couldn't stand it if you cried."

She blinked rapidly a few times to dry her tears before they had a chance to fall.

"Don't flatter yourself," she said as harshly as she could. "You're not worth crying over."

"Because I didn't tell you everything about myself?" He looked pained. "I was going to. This afternoon at the carriage house. You know that."

"How do I know that?" Anger gave fuel to her voice. "Because you asked me to trust you? Why should I do that?"

"Because I love you," he said softly.

He moved closer to her and this time she couldn't step away without stepping into a urinal. He reached up a hand to frame her face, and she was powerless to bat it away. Just as she was powerless to evade his kiss.

He cupped her head to hold it in place but there was nothing forceful about his kiss. His lips were soft and coaxing, asking her without words to open to him.

God help her, she did. She couldn't stop herself, not when she would crave his touch until the end of her days. The kiss was bittersweet, coaxing a response from her that had tears streaming down her cheeks. He must have felt them on his face because he drew back and brushed them away with the pads of his fingers.

"I love you," he repeated, fastening eyes on her that looked open and honest.

She closed her own eyes in mortification at the way she'd not only responded to him but the way her body still trembled with suppressed desire.

Honest?

How could she possibly connect that word to Chance? And how could he speak of love when he was standing there with his law degree and his expensive suit?

"You don't know the first thing about love," she said in a shaky voice. "Love isn't built on lies. It grows out of mutual respect and trust."

"So I could have trusted you not to bolt if I'd told you right off the bat I was a lawyer from D.C.?"

When she didn't answer, he continued, his breath soft and sweet against her cheek. "Can't you see I didn't tell you about myself because I was afraid I'd lose you?"

She felt the tears threaten again and squeezed her eyes shut until she had them under control. Then she shook her head.

"That doesn't excuse it." Her voice gained strength. "That doesn't make what you did any less appalling."

"I hoped it would make it more understandable."

Tiffany lifted her chin and narrowed her eyes, steeling herself against the hope and the pain on his face. "I can't understand somebody I don't know."

The squeaking sound of the door and the click of heels on the marble floor alerted them they were no longer alone, but neither of them broke eye contact.

"Maybe I don't have to go all that bad after all."

The loud proclamation seemed to unfreeze Tiffany's muscles. She fastened her hands around Chance's wrists and drew them away from her face.

"That's okay." She addressed the man but kept her gaze on Chance. "We're done here."

She ignored Chance's pained look and wrenched out of his arms, promising herself as she walked out of the bathroom door that she was also walking out of his life.

Forever.

13

CHANCE'S EXPENSIVE LEATHER shoes sank into the rich green carpeting of the prestigious law firm as he made his way down the hall toward a familiar office.

The surprise, even to himself, was that the office was in Atlanta rather than Washington, D.C.

"Chance McMann, as I live and litigate." A slender, white-haired man heading toward him reached out to give him a quick handshake but kept on walking. "Tired of that D.C. firm already?"

"I'm only here for a visit," Chance called after him but the man had already disappeared around a corner.

That's the way it was at The Atlanta Group. Nobody stopped and smelled the roses. The most they had time for was a quick sniff on the way past.

Life wasn't any less hectic at his new law firm although Chance had noticed an important difference. Hustle wasn't valued nearly as much as the ability to rack up billable hours.

A secretary had already announced his arrival over an intercom so Chance rapped three times on the door to his father's office before opening it.

"Hello, Dad."

William McMann lifted his head from the legal

briefs he was examining, removed his fashionable, wire-rimmed reading glasses and got to his feet.

"Chauncy," he said in the booming baritone that used to make Chance quake in his athletic shoes when he was growing up. "This is quite a surprise."

Chance might have embraced his father if he'd been within reach but William McMann stayed put behind the desk. He bent at the waist, stretching his hand over the gleaming mahogany desktop for a shake.

Chance took his father's hand while he noted that at fifty-nine William McMann still exuded the strength and confidence of a much-younger man.

Shorter than Chance by a few inches, the elder McMann gave the illusion of height with erect posture and a strict exercise regimen that kept his body lean. His hairdresser helped him retain the illusion of youth by discreetly coloring the gray in his dark hair.

As soon as they were through shaking hands, William McMann settled into his leather wing chair, giving Chance the uncomfortable feeling that he was a client.

"Care to tell me why you have a black eye?"

Chance brought a hand to his face, surprised that he'd forgotten about the injury. "It's nothing," he said. "I bumped into something, is all."

His father's mouth twisted, but surprisingly he didn't press, probably because he had a busy day on slate. "Then care to tell me what brings you here?"

Chance had been asking himself the same question since that morning at the Savannah airport when he'd impulsively booked a flight to Atlanta instead of D.C.

He wondered what his father would say if he told him he figured home was the best place to lick his wounds.

He'd made a crucial mistake in not considering that Tiffany and Mary, both congressman's daughters, might know each other. Still, he hadn't counted on Tiffany throwing his declaration of love back in his face. She'd done so with such vehemence, he still felt as though he'd just been slapped.

The hell of it was that he didn't blame her for not believing he loved her. Why should she when he'd been nothing but a fraud from the first time she saw him?

Would his father have sympathy for his broken heart? Or would he claim Chance had gotten what he deserved for pretending to be something he was not?

In the book of law according to William McMann, nothing was better than being a hard-driving, success-grasping attorney.

"I was in the area and thought I'd stop for a visit," Chance said instead of any of the things running through his mind.

The corners of William McMann's usually impassive mouth turned downward into a frown.

"You should have warned us. You know how busy things are at this time of year. Your brother's in Dallas speaking at a medical convention and your mother and I have dinner plans with the deputy mayor and his wife." He tapped a pencil on the desk. "I couldn't possibly cancel, not when I need him to talk to the mayor about the proposed tax incentives to lure business to the area."

"I wouldn't dream of asking you to cancel." Chance schooled his expression to remain neutral. For as long as he could remember, his father always had plans. Some of them involved Chance's future, but more often they had nothing to do with him. He made a snap decision. "I'm catching the next plane out after I stop by the courthouse. I'm hoping Mother's docket isn't so full she won't have time for lunch."

"Very good," William McMann said and pinned him with a steely-eyed stare. "Now suppose you tell me what you're really doing here."

"I already told you. I'm in town for a visit."

"Did something go wrong with that case involving Jake Greeley's daughter? Are you here to break the bad news to me in person?"

"There was no case," Chance said. "The woman never hired a lawyer to file one. All she was after was money."

"Greeley paid her, right?"

"He probably would have done anything to keep the allegation out of the papers that his daughter had been drinking and driving."

"So what's the problem?" His father's eyes narrowed. "Don't tell me you refused to settle the case out of court."

"Why would it be so terrible if I had?" Chance asked.

"Because I told Jake Greeley you'd handle it." His father's voice spiked. "For God's sake, Chauncy, do you know how valuable it is for the firm to have a friend in Congress? I was counting on you."

"Relax, Dad, I made the payment."

He watched the tension drain from his father like a balloon with a leak. "I don't understand." William McMann made a sweeping gesture with his hand. "If you made the payment, what's this about?"

"I suppose I was thinking aloud," Chance said slowly. "Mary Greeley wasn't drinking and driving. It was a lie the other woman made up. But Jake Greeley's priority wasn't the truth. It was keeping the story out of the papers. All he cared about was appearances."

His father huffed. "So what's the problem? Appearances are important. You understand that."

The sad truth was that Chance did understand and had for far too long.

He'd been keeping up appearances his entire life: Getting into the right schools, wearing the right clothes, joining the right law firms.

The only time he'd ever let down his guard had been with Tiffany. That was the only time he'd felt free to be himself. Too bad it had all been a lie. Unless, he thought with sudden insight, it hadn't been.

"*This* is the lie," he exclaimed under his breath.

"Excuse me, son. I'm not following you." William McMann screwed up his broad forehead so that deep lines intersected it. "Did you say something about a lie?"

"Yes." Chance nodded. How could he have believed that he was suited for the stuffy existence he'd been leading? More important, why had he let it happen?

"I've been lying to myself," he said in a soft voice.

"Lying about what?" The elder McMann seemed completely mystified. "If you're in trouble, son, tell me now. Does it have something to do with that black eye? No matter. I have friends in high places. Whatever it is doesn't have to be a crisis."

"I'm not in that kind of trouble," Chance said.

"Something's not right." William McMann pounded the desk with his fist. "I can feel it."

"Let me ask you something, Dad," Chance said, walking closer to the desk. "Why didn't you take me seriously when I said I wanted to work in a D.A.'s office?"

"I did take you seriously. That's why I discouraged you."

"But why?"

"You know why. A lawyer deserves a certain status in life. Not to mention being richly rewarded for his efforts."

"What if those things didn't matter to me?"

"Those things matter to everybody," his father said impatiently.

They probably mattered to Tiffany's congressman father, which would partly explain why she'd become a lobbyist.

Yet last night, when she still believed him to be a nomad, Tiffany had been ready to leave her moneyed, prestigious life behind to be with him.

If only Chance had the strength of character to follow her lead and go after what he wanted instead of what his father wanted for him. If only he were the man she'd thought him to be.

He remembered the soft look that had come into Tiffany's dark eyes when she told him she admired him for having the courage to live his life his way.

Chance hadn't been worthy of her admiration then, but that didn't mean he couldn't be.

"You asked me why I'd come home," Chance said thoughtfully. His father nodded, apprehension etched on his strong features.

"I thought I'd come home to heal, but that's not it." Before his father could ask what he needed to heal from, Chance plowed ahead. "I came home to tell you I'm through pretending to be someone I'm not. It's time I made some changes in my life."

William McMann's face distorted with alarm. "What kind of changes?"

"That depends on what happens when I see a certain woman in Savannah," Chance said and headed for the door.

"But you need to get back to D.C."

"Oh, no," Chance said, understanding himself for the first time in a long time. Maybe in forever. "I need to go to Savannah. D.C. was a detour."

"Chauncy McMann, you come back here and explain what you're talking about."

His father's voice drifted after him but for once in his life Chance didn't listen to it.

It was past time he listened to his heart instead.

THE SAVANNAH SUN disappeared behind a cloud, throwing the historic square Tiffany and Susie were walking through in shadow.

Tiffany thought the disappearing sun pretty much summarized her visit to the city, because the joy had gone out of it after she'd discovered Chance's deception.

Determinedly affixing a bright smile on her face, she linked her arm through Susie's. She refused to shed another tear over that man. Whoever he was.

"Didn't you think the she-crab soup at lunch was fabulous?" she asked Susie. "The only thing better was the company."

"You didn't have to treat me." Susie squeezed her arm. "But I won't pretend I'm not glad you did."

"It was the least I could do after you let me stay in your carriage house. I only wish we'd been able to spend more time together."

"Me, too. But you had a good time with Chance, right?"

The question hung in the air between them like bait on a hook. It had been two days since Tiffany had discovered Chance for what he was but she'd yet to confide in Susie.

She didn't want to think about Chance, let alone talk about him. Not when the pain of his betrayal still sliced deep.

"It was okay," Tiffany said, striving to sound offhanded.

"Okay?" Susie repeated, shaking her head so her

blond curls danced. "Since when does a sizzling affair with a hot man rank as merely okay?"

"Since we decided never to see each other again," Tiffany stated, uncomfortably aware that was what *she* had decided.

Chance, the bastard, had professed to love her. If she'd given him the opportunity, he might even have declared that he wanted to spend the rest of his life with her.

"You what?" Susie stopped walking and turned rounded eyes to her.

"Never mind about that," Tiffany said with false brightness. "Why don't you tell me what's next for the tourism bureau now that this year's festival is over?

"Has your boss ever considered hiring a branding firm? It's a hot concept that's moving into the tourism industry. The branding firm does an audit of how the city's perceived as a travel destination and suggests ways to give it a claim of distinction."

"That's an interesting idea, but you're nuts if you think I'm letting you change the subject that easily." Susie's usually pert mouth had a stubborn set. "Tell me what happened between you and Chance."

"Nothing happened."

"One minute you're sleeping with him and the next you won't talk about him. Sounds to me like something happened."

Tiffany unlinked her elbow from Susie's and crossed both of her arms protectively over her chest.

"Here today, gone tomorrow," Tiffany quipped. "You know how it is."

"That's not how it is with you," Susie said. "I could have sworn that wasn't the way it was with him either. That's why I stopped worrying about you. I thought you two were falling in love."

"Love?" Tiffany tried to laugh but what escaped sounded more like a hiccuping sob. "How could I be in love with a man like that? His name isn't even Chance. It's Chauncy."

Susie grabbed her hand and pulled her over to a park bench strategically situated under a magnificent elm tree. A squirrel jumped playfully from one of the tree's branches to the next, bringing tears to Tiffany's eyes.

It wasn't fair that anything should be so happy when she was so miserable.

"Sit," Susie said in a voice that allowed for no argument. "Then tell me what happened."

Fifteen minutes later, Susie let out a long breath.

"Let me see if I understand this correctly," she said. "You're angry at Chance because he's a lawyer who wears expensive suits."

Tiffany shook her head vigorously. "I'm angry because he lied to me."

"About what?"

"He's no good-time guy," Tiffany declared.

"He seemed like he was having a pretty good time to me."

Tiffany frowned because she supposed that was true. For an attorney who spent most of his life in a suit, he seemed to enjoy himself when he wasn't wearing one.

"That's not the point. A lie's still a lie if it's a lie of omission. He had lots of chances to tell me who he really was and he didn't take any of them."

"Excuse me, ladies, could you spare some change?"

They'd been so deep in conversation that Tiffany hadn't seen the man's approach. She looked up, then immediately wished she hadn't.

Everything but the whites of the man's eyes was green, and there was a lot of everything to see.

It wasn't quite as warm today as it had been the previous week, probably no more than seventy degrees, but the man seemed perfectly comfortable in his clinging green bathing suit. She figured the green paint coating every generous inch of him must be keeping him warm.

Before she could reach inside her purse for her wallet, the man raised a hand. "I don't expect something for nothing."

He put a harmonica to his lips and played a surprisingly recognizable Irish tune. Tiffany resisted the urge to plaster her back against the park bench and kept her face carefully neutral until his performance was over.

"That was great," Susie said while she clapped her hands, "but St. Patrick's Day is over."

"Aye, I know that," the man said, sticking the dollar bills they gave him in the waistband of his bathing suit, "but it's hard to give up a good gig when you find one."

He was still playing the harmonica when he left

them. Susie laughed as she watched him go but Tiffany let out a relieved breath.

"He made you uncomfortable," Susie observed.

"Of course he did. He was a nearly naked green man playing the harmonica."

Susie grew silent, appearing to be deep in thought.

"Remember when I said the wild Savannah didn't suit you?" she finally asked, and Tiffany nodded. "You pretended it did, just like you pretended that man didn't make you nervous."

"So what?" Tiffany blew out a breath. "Most of the time, I pretend I like living in Washington, D.C., and being a lobbyist, too."

"Exactly."

Tiffany shook her head, which was starting to throb. "I don't know what point you're trying to make."

"Neither do I," Susie said with a helpless shrug. She took Tiffany's hand and squeezed it. "I'm not the most insightful person around but it seems to me all that pretending you've been doing must mean *something*."

She raised herself off the bench, waving off Tiffany's half-hearted attempt to do the same.

"No, don't get up. I have to get back to the office but you should stay here and enjoy the park. It is your last day in Savannah."

Blowing her a kiss, Susie walked off, leaving Tiffany alone with her jumbled thoughts.

With the St. Patrick's Day festival crowds gone, the city had resorted to its usual serene self. Susie was right. The conservative Savannah's tranquil, moss-draped beauty appealed to her on a visceral level even if she had pretended to prefer the other one.

She frowned, not sure that was relevant. So what if she'd professed to enjoy riding on the back of a motorcycle, taking a dip in the frigid ocean water and running in the rain?

Everybody pretended to be something they weren't at one time or another. She'd been doing it her entire life.

Then why, a little voice in the back of her head piped up, had she gotten so angry at Chance for pretending to be something he wasn't? Why had she held him up to an impossible standard she herself couldn't meet?

"Oh, no," Tiffany said aloud, bringing her hands to her flushed cheeks.

She'd gotten so good at pretending to be someone she wasn't that she'd driven Chance away. All along, the only place she'd ever felt comfortable being herself was in his arms.

How could she have been such a hypocrite?

More important, how could she have let the man she loved go without a fight?

She sprang up from the bench and hurried in the direction of the carriage house, praying it wasn't too late to right her wrong.

Two businessmen in suits walked by, reminding her of her life in Washington, D.C. A shudder passed through her because if she'd learned one thing about herself, it was that she didn't want to go back to that life.

But staying in Savannah wasn't an option, not if Chance found it in his heart to forgive her.

She'd do anything to make things up to him, even don panty hose and attend political fund-raisers with rooms full of Starched Suits for the rest of her life.

Because she'd finally realized it wasn't the suit upon the man that mattered.

It was the man inside the suit.

14

CHANCE KEPT HIS CHIN HIGH and his eyes straight ahead, but he couldn't escape the feeling the other passengers in the airport terminal were staring at him.

He chanced a quick look around only to discover that nobody was paying him much attention. The air went out of his lungs.

He should have expected as much. Savannah was a gracious Southern city, populated by residents who counted good manners among their attributes.

"You've got to be kidding me."

His eyes swung back around to a middle-aged woman emerging from a gift shop that sold books and newspapers. She reminded him of his mother without the judge's robe, refined speech patterns and the tact.

"Irish you would kiss me," she read off his kelly-green T-shirt before throwing back her head and laughing. "A good-looking young fellow like you and that's the best line you can come up with?"

He gave her a tight smile. She couldn't possibly be one of those good-mannered, gracious Southerners he'd been silently praising.

Nope. This lady had to be a tourist.

"It worked once," he told her.

"Then you're one lucky son of a gun," the woman

said, still chuckling as she went to pass him, "because I can't imagine it working again."

Chance walked on, not quite as sure of his course of action as when he'd boarded the plane in Atlanta that afternoon.

He'd put the ridiculous shirt back on to prove to Tiffany that he could be the man she wanted him to be. But maybe his father was at least partly right about appearances mattering.

Appearances mattered when they didn't give others an accurate impression of what was inside you.

Chance did want to make changes but he wasn't so unconventional that he felt comfortable wearing a shirt that invited kisses from strangers.

He was a lawyer, for Pete's sake. Not only that, he liked being a lawyer. He even enjoyed wearing good-looking suits.

The revelations gave him pause.

Had this been a bad idea? Was he coming to Tiffany under false pretenses? Was it impossible for him to be the good-time guy she wanted?

He looked up to heaven, wishing a divine force could give him the answers, but all he saw was the ceiling of the terminal.

"At least give me a sign," he muttered before bringing his gaze back down. It locked on a tall, well-dressed brunette who was hurrying through the terminal wearing a royal-blue power suit that screamed class, wealth and privilege.

Tiffany.

And just like that, he had the answers to all those difficult questions.

For a future with Tiffany, he could do anything.

IF SHE DIDN'T HURRY, Tiffany thought as she sped through the airport terminal, she'd miss the last D.C.-bound flight out of Savannah.

And if she missed the flight, she'd have to wait an extra twelve hours to apologize to Chance.

Twelve hours. It might as well be a lifetime.

She couldn't wait that long.

She could hardly wait as long as it would take the plane to get to Washington, D.C.

She didn't know where Chance lived but a staffer in Congressman Greeley's office had given her the address of his law firm. She intended to head there as soon as the plane landed.

It was nearly dark now and would be darker still when she got to D.C. but she knew how the city worked. Lots of lawyers didn't leave their buildings until well into the night. She'd prefer if Chance wasn't among the workaholic masses, but she'd take him any way she could get him.

She'd even take him as a mirage in the middle of the terminal wearing the "Irish You Would Kiss Me" shirt.

She was about to blow by the hallucination in her zeal to get to the real thing when it spoke her name.

"Tiffany."

She put on the brakes so fast she almost fell off her high heels. Mirages couldn't speak. She blinked but neither did the mirage disappear, which meant the Chance in the terminal was flesh and blood. Her pulse sped up.

"Chance," she breathed, walking toward him as though he were a magnet and she an iron particle. She didn't stop until she could have reached out and touched him, but she didn't. Not with so much misunderstanding between them. "What are you doing here?"

She held her breath as she waited for his answer, afraid to hope that his presence in the airport had anything to do with her. Maybe he hadn't left Savannah days before as she'd supposed. Maybe he was just leaving now.

"I was coming to find you," he said, and her heart soared so high she felt it in her throat.

The air between them crackled as they stared at each other but the silence lengthened. Tiffany started to ask why he was looking for her but her courage failed her at the last moment.

"Why are you wearing that shirt?" she asked instead.

He scratched his head and that strong chin she loved quivered. "I guess I'm trying to make a point."

"Which is?" she prompted.

"I wanted to convince you that I'm not a Starched Suit."

"Why?" she asked, hardly daring to breathe.

He pinched the bridge of his nose, covering the little bump she loved so well. "Ah, hell. I was going to tell you it's because I can be that good-time guy you want me to be. But the truth is I feel like a fool wearing this T-shirt."

He shifted his feet and swallowed. Then he threw up his hands, the look on his face so pained that Tiffany hurt.

"I can only be what I am," he said softly, his blue-green eyes locked on hers. "The guy who loves you."

The lump in her throat was so large that for a moment Tiffany couldn't speak.

"I know I misled you," he said, his eyes burning into hers. "Hell, I don't even play the sax. I used to. I'd like to again. But I don't play it now. I wouldn't blame you if you told me to get lost again but I'm praying you won't. Take another chance on me, Tiffany. Please."

He looked so hopeful that Tiffany's chest clenched. She made a supreme effort to clear her throat because it was important that she tell him what was in her heart.

"I don't need to." She blinked back tears of happiness. "The first chance I took already paid off, because I love you, too."

The awed look on his face stole her breath. "Do you mean it?"

"With all my heart," she said, smiling now. She made a point of looking down at his chest. "Do you mean that?"

His grin turned rakish when he realized her meaning. "Oh, yeah," he said. "Irish you would."

Then she was in his arms, her lips wildly connecting with any part of his face they could reach. He chuckled and found her mouth with his, but it felt to Tiffany as though he'd found her heart instead.

For endless moments, the terminal seemed to disappear along with the other passengers. Her feelings were so overwhelming, so impossible to contain, that Tiffany would have kept on kissing him if he hadn't drawn back.

Only then did she become aware of the stream of passengers arcing around them, the intercom voices announcing flight arrivals and departures and the middle-aged woman openly staring at them.

"Well, I'll be darned," she said to Chance. "That gimmick of yours did too work a second time."

A HALF HOUR LATER, Chance breathed in the fragrant Southern air after the driver of the cab he and Tiffany had taken from the airport pulled away.

They were in residential Savannah, near a bed of azaleas and in front of the carriage house where they'd fallen in love, but the night was so beautiful that Chance was in no hurry to go indoors.

"There's one thing you still haven't told me," he said, taking Tiffany's hand and sliding his thumb over her palm. "Why were you at the airport? I thought you weren't leaving until tomorrow."

"I was flying home to you," she said simply.

The sentiment behind her comment warmed him but the way she'd called Washington, D.C., home left him cold. He had yet to form an attachment to the city and doubted he ever could.

But if that's where Tiffany was, that's where he

wanted to be. Even if it meant staying at Whitaker, Baker and Taft.

He watched her dark gaze sweep over the historic buildings around them and arc toward the sky. The night was enchanting in the way only a Southern night could be, with the stars winking down on the city as if to say it was favored.

"I'll miss Savannah when we leave to start our life together," she whispered.

Chance hardly dared breathe. Could he be understanding her correctly? "You say that as though you'd like to live here."

"I would," she said, then laid a hand on his arm, her expression earnest. "But I'll be happy in D.C. I'll try to understand how many hours you work. I'll smile at the Starched Suits when we go to political affairs. I'll even take your suits to the dry cleaners." She gave a little laugh. "I'd do anything for you, Chance McMann."

"Would you move to Savannah?"

Her eyes widened and her mouth parted. "Are you serious?"

"As serious as I've ever been in my life." He rubbed the backs of his knuckles against the smooth skin of her cheek. "What do you think?"

"I think I'd love it here. I even know where I'd like to work. At the tourism bureau with Susie. Since I got here, I've had lots of ideas about promoting the city. Which isn't all that different from promoting milk and cheese but a lot more fun. And Susie mentioned at lunch today that there's going to be an opening soon."

She stopped abruptly, making an obvious effort to contain the enthusiasm he found so charming. "But what about you? You have a good job in D.C."

"It's not the job I want," he said and took her by the shoulders. "You made me understand that, Tiffany. I've been trying to please my father for so long I didn't realize I wasn't pleasing myself."

"I know the feeling," she said wryly.

"I'd like to switch to criminal law and work in the D.A.'s office, which is something I've always wanted," he said. "But if that doesn't work out, I could always practice law on a smaller scale."

"Would that be enough for you?"

He gave a vigorous nod. "I found out this weekend I'm not as much of a Starched Suit as I thought. I don't want to work my life away to impress other people. Success is relative. To me, it's being able to make the time to run in the rain, swim in the ice-cold ocean and ride a motorcycle."

"Maybe I'm not wild enough for you then," Tiffany said, sounding unsure of herself. "Because I have a confession to make. I hate those things."

He laughed. "Don't you think I know that?"

"You do?" Her mouth parted. "And that doesn't bother you?"

"Not a bit. There are plenty of things we can do together that we'll both enjoy," he said, then lifted his eyebrows, "including my favorite."

"What's that?" she asked, but he could tell she already knew the answer by the sensuous smile she gave him.

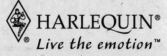

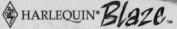

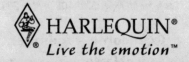

eHARLEQUIN.com

Becoming an eHarlequin.com member is easy,
fun and **FREE!** Join today to enjoy great benefits:

- **Super savings** on all our books, including
  members-only discounts and offers!

- Enjoy **exclusive online reads**—FREE!

- Info, tips and **expert advice** on writing
  your own romance novel.

- FREE romance **newsletters,**
  customized by you!

- Find out the latest on your
  favorite authors.

- Enter to win exciting **contests
  and promotions!**

- Chat with other members in our
  community message boards!

**Plus, we'll send you 2 FREE Internet-exclusive
eHarlequin.com books (no strings!)
just to say thanks for joining us online.**

**To become a member,
visit www.eHarlequin.com today!**

If you enjoyed what you just read,
then we've got an offer you can't resist!

Take 2 bestselling
love stories FREE!
Plus get a FREE surprise gift!

Clip this page and mail it to Harlequin Reader Service®

IN U.S.A.	IN CANADA
3010 Walden Ave.	P.O. Box 609
P.O. Box 1867	Fort Erie, Ontario
Buffalo, N.Y. 14240-1867	L2A 5X3

YES! Please send me 2 free Harlequin Temptation® novels and my free surprise gift. After receiving them, if I don't wish to receive anymore, I can return the shipping statement marked cancel. If I don't cancel, I will receive 4 brand-new novels each month, before they're available in stores. In the U.S.A., bill me at the bargain price of $3.57 plus 25¢ shipping and handling per book and applicable sales tax, if any*. In Canada, bill me at the bargain price of $4.24 plus 25¢ shipping and handling per book and applicable taxes**. That's the complete price and a savings of 10% off the cover prices—what a great deal! I understand that accepting the 2 free books and gift places me under no obligation ever to buy any books. I can always return a shipment and cancel at any time. Even if I never buy another book from Harlequin, the 2 free books and gift are mine to keep forever.

142 HDN DNT5
342 HDN DNT6

Name	(PLEASE PRINT)	
Address	Apt.#	
City	State/Prov.	Zip/Postal Code

* Terms and prices subject to change without notice. Sales tax applicable in N.Y.
** Canadian residents will be charged applicable provincial taxes and GST.
  All orders subject to approval. Offer limited to one per household and not valid to
  current Harlequin Temptation® subscribers.
  ® are registered trademarks of Harlequin Enterprises Limited.

TEMP02   ©1998 Harlequin Enterprises Limited

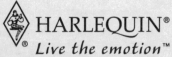

HARLEQUIN®
Temptation

AMERICAN HEROES

These men are heroes—
strong, fearless...
And impossible to resist!

Join bestselling authors Lori Foster, Donna Kauffman
and Jill Shalvis as they deliver up

MEN OF COURAGE

Harlequin anthology
May 2003

Followed by *American Heroes* miniseries
in Harlequin Temptation

RILEY by Lori Foster
June 2003

SEAN by Donna Kauffman
July 2003

LUKE by Jill Shalvis
August 2003

Don't miss this sexy new miniseries by some of
Temptation's hottest authors!

Available at your favorite retail outlet.

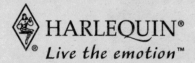

HARLEQUIN®
Live the emotion™

Visit us at www.eHarlequin.com

HTAH